The Targeting of
Robert Alvar

The Targeting of Robert Alvar

JANE MORELL

ROBERT HALE · LONDON

ISBN 0 7090 6319 9

Robert Hale Limited
Clerkenwell House
Clerkenwell Green
London EC1R 0HT

2 4 6 8 10 9 7 5 3 1

Typeset in North Wales by
Derek Doyle & Associates, Mold, Flintshire.
Printed in Great Britain by
St Edmundsbury Press, Bury St Edmunds, Suffolk.
Bound by WBC Book Manufacturers Limited, Bridgend.

To all those who patrol the frontiers they believe in.

My first thought was that he had committed a crime, but soon I saw it was only a passion that had moved into his body like a stranger.

A View From the Bridge Arthur Miller

Off the Record

'Ten years you've been working at this, and what have you achieved?' Curtis sat back in his chair, staring across his desk at his tall rangily built visitor.

'Three drug barons dead by my own hand. I rate that pretty fair going.'

'Nevertheless their trade continues to flourish.'

'It gives me considerable satisfaction that those three at least have paid the price.'

'But to our certain knowledge, in a matter of days three others, no less competent and certainly no less ruthless, took their places.'

'True.' Hal Shearer smoothed back his grey-streaked dark hair and smiled at the police superintendent, Jack Curtis, his close friend of more than twenty years' standing; but it was a tight-lipped, narrow smile and served merely to accentuate the bitterness etched into his saturnine face. 'Maybe, though, God willing, each one of those three new men sleeps less easily because of what happened to his predecessors, some nights at least,' he went on, a cold violence in his voice. 'I'm happy with what I do, Jack, and I intend to continue with it.' He paused. 'I'm forty-eight now. Given luck, I'll double my "score" in the course of the next few years.'

Curtis eyed him broodingly, knowing he had lost the argument – as so often before. 'Well,' he observed after a moment, 'there's no denying it, if you take out Robert Alvar you'll be doing a lot of decent folk a great favour.'

'Alvar's no worse than the rest of them.'

'Granted. You'll never run out of targets.'

'I don't expect to.' Again Shearer gave his sardonic smile. 'That depends on how long *I* live, I suppose,' he added. 'Maybe one of these days one of them will smell me out, finger me for what I am. I wouldn't last long after that.'

1

Shearer parked his hired Mercedes a short distance from the entrance to the Meridien Hotel in Barcelona at 8.15 in the evening. As on the previous four days, he positioned the car so that he would be able to spot his quarry when the man emerged from the hotel to take his customary pre-dinner walk. Walk, not stroll: at sixty-three years of age Robert Alvar prided himself on his physical fitness. He worked at that with the same sort – if not the same degree – of wholeheartedness that he devoted to running his Europe-wide organization for the import and distribution of illegal drugs acquired through its South American affiliations.

The rapidly increasing growth of that organization was why, eight months earlier, Shearer had decided to go after Alvar next. As on the previous occasions when he had selected a target and gone for it, he was taking his time. Hold your fire until the perfect opportunity presents itself, then you'll get away with murder: that was Shearer's guiding principle. Rigidly adhered to throughout each of the three similar missions he had carried out over the last ten years, it had proved one hundred per cent effective.

Behind the wheel of the Mercedes, his strong-boned face set and purposeful, his cold grey eyes checking the identity of each man who emerged through the impressive glass-and-chrome doors of the Meridien, Shearer watched and waited for Alvar. While he did so, he ran his mind over how things stood with his present mission. Having been working for the last fortnight in different locations in Europe – Holland, Belgium, Greece – the three top guns of Alvar's consortium had come to stay at the hotel in order to discuss and collate the results of their separate initiatives.

Bossman of the syndicate was Robert Alvar, born Roberto Alvarez. A native of Colombia, he was an astute and formidably ruthless user and, when necessary, destroyer of men. Second to him in power was his niece-by-marriage, Elena Fuentes, elevated to that position four years earlier following the death of her husband Carlos, Alvar's nephew, blown apart by a grenade in the course of a police raid in Rio de Janeiro. Lastly, there was Ramon Gutierrez, younger than either, very much the junior partner at present but, according to reports, extremely ambitious. Elena Fuentes was said to be jealous of his increasing prestige with Alvar, but trying to keep the fact hidden from him.

That particular evening's possible opportunity to kill Alvar had presented itself to Shearer out of the blue. A couple of days before he was due to fly out to Barcelona for a week on company business – his fifth such trip since the beginning of the year – Jack Curtis had telephoned him at his head office in London and informed him of this planned meeting of Alvar and his associates.

I might get a chance against the bastard over there, you never know your luck, Shearer had told himself then. Don't look gift horses in the mouth, just make sure you're ready to ride one if he turns up.

So, on arriving in Barcelona, he had used various long-established contacts in the city to purchase a handgun and silencer on the black market, in hope more than in expectation. So far his luck had been out, apart from one close call which had occurred the very first night he'd shadowed Alvar on his pre-dinner walk. Suddenly then, Alvar had turned a corner. Covertly, Shearer had followed him on foot – to find the two of them proceeding, alone together, along a poorly lit alley between high walls set with small frosted windows and three or four street-level garage doors. At once he'd marked his own exit-run, drawn the silenced weapon from his pocket, set himself, taken aim – but on the instant one of the doors ahead of him had burst open, three men had spilled out drunkenly into the alley and his chance was gone. None had offered since then and this was the last night Alvar would spend in the city; he and Gutierrez were scheduled to return to London the next day, Elena to fly to Rome. . . .

Shearer leaned forward, peering out through the windscreen. Alvar had appeared at the doors of the hotel, was standing talking to the commissionaire. I'd know Robert Alvar anywhere, the arrogant bastard, Shearer thought balefully, his eyes riveted on the trim, erect figure. He's five feet seven inches tall, his hair's straight and thick and snowy white and, given luck this evening, I'll gun him down—

No, God rot him, I damn well shan't! Shearer swore. The glass doors of the Meridien had opened again and a slim, dark-haired woman had stepped out, hatless, a light jacket over her darkish calf-length skirt. Alvar turned to her as she came up to him and the two of them went on together across the paved forecourt of the hotel and joined passers-by on the pavement. Shearer studied them as they walked away from him. He knew the woman to be Danielle Fraser, Alvar's trusted PA, but this was the first time he had seen her at all clearly. Not that he could glean much about her looks now: he saw simply a well-dressed young woman with shoulder-length hair who was about the same height as Alvar. Nevertheless, that evening, watching her as she walked at Alvar's side, Shearer perceived that Danielle Fraser moved most beautifully, with a lissom, subtle grace; he was very aware of her. But he cursed her for her presence at Alvar's side that night.

As soon as the two of them were out of sight, he drove out of the city, taking a minor coast-hugging road to a place he had discovered months earlier. Traffic was light, so when, some twenty minutes later, he pulled into the small lay-by he had taken note of before, he had no need to bide his time. He took the gun out from under the dashboard, fitted on its silencer and slipped it into his pocket. Then he got out, crossed the road and stood at the edge of the cliff, looking out across the darkening sea. At his feet, the land dropped sheer for thirty feet to a cruelly rocky shore. Deep water there. A left-to-right glance along the road behind him showed it still empty of traffic so he pulled out the gun and, with a swift, powerful side-arm action, hurled it far out to sea.

I knew tonight's try was a thousand-to-one chance right from the start, but it seemed worth giving it a go, he thought as he drove back to the city. No sweat, though. Much the same sort of thing happened on two of my previous strikes. But every time I go into action I'm ready and able to abort it at a second's notice; I'm the only one working at the sharp end so I can simply let it go, walk away. . . . Well, six weeks ago I started in on the groundwork for a strike against you in England, Alvar, at a place a few miles outside Sutton. Soon as I get back there I'll have it up and running. That's home territory for me. You'll not escape me then.

'Stop baiting the boy, Elena!' Smoothing back his white hair, pushing himself up out of his armchair, Alvar glared across at the elegant blonde woman seated on the sofa opposite him in her suite at the Meridien, a glass of *pisco* sour in one hand (the white-rum cocktail, her favourite drink, and mixed to perfection by Alvar himself, proportions of whipped egg white and lemon juice exactly to her taste). 'Ramon is handling our new deal with our collaborators in Customs at Bristol extremely well; there is no call for sarcastic comment from you!'

She shrugged, then turned her head away from the young and handsome Ramon Gutierrez who was standing, fuming, on Alvar's right, and settled back into the cushions. 'If you say so, Roberto,' she murmured, smiling. 'Please, go ahead; complete his briefing. I shall hold my peace, and enjoy my *pisco*.'

It was eight o'clock in the evening of their last day in Barcelona. The sitting-room was stylishly appointed, its colours gold and cream, with touches of crimson. Its curtains were drawn, and shaded lamps and concealed lighting suffused it with a warm glow that was kind to the faces of the four people gathered there.

Standing beside the drinks trolley by the windows, her slate-coloured business suit immaculate, dark hair glossy, eyes expressionless, Danielle Fraser continued to behave as she had since the meeting began two hours earlier: she remained silent unless spoken to, but all the while took careful note of what passed between these three directors of the Alvar consortium, both spoken and unspoken. As confidential PA to Robert Alvar, appointed to that highly sensitive job by him personally as a result of special circumstances, her place on the edge of their inner circle gave her considerable latent influence but no definitive voice in decision-making.

The person she observed most closely was Elena Fuentes, who for twelve years had been an active business partner to her husband, Carlos, Alvar's greatly beloved nephew and right-hand man in his drug-trafficking operations. On Carlos's death she had asked to be allowed to take his place in the top echelon of the organization and, for his dead nephew's sake and because she had proved herself as informed and ruthless as he in the innermost workings of the business, Alvar had agreed. Danielle disliked Elena intensely, and had for some time been aware that her dislike was built on a gut feeling somewhere between apprehension and fear. Recognizing its importance to herself, she had given it considerable thought, but had been unable to discover any tangible reason for its existence. Since she began working for Alvar she had learned a great deal about Elena: a striking woman, yes, but she had a vicious temper which she often found difficult to control. She was also clever, habitually devious and frequently a vicious user of other people. All those judgements were true, Danielle was certain of that, and because of it knew she had to be extremely cautious in her dealings with the woman. But they did not explain the apprehension in her and, unable to explain it, she was haunted by a foreboding that, one day and with terrible suddenness, she *would* be able to explain it – but by then it would be too late, her cover would be blown.

Alvar ended his briefing of Ramon with a warning to be wary of Johnson, front man of the four-strong cadre now on their payroll in Bristol. Johnson knew he was extremely valuable to Alvar, and he would be sure to try to trade on that when cash payments came to be decided between Gutierrez and himself.

'You will hold the man to the amount on offer,' Alvar said finally. Then he sat down in his chair again, turned to Elena and brought up the last item on their agenda. He had deliberately left it until last because he knew it would infuriate her. 'There is one other matter before we go our separate ways for the evening,' he said to her. 'I have decided to take only Danielle with me to the meeting at Langley Manor in three weeks' time—'

'*Why?*' Elena was on her feet, confronting him, blue eyes blazing. '*I* was to accompany you! I am second in command, it is for me to take part in the negotiations with Der Broeck! Of course we need Danielle there, I accept that, but I insist on being present!'

'No, Elena.' Alvar continued to sit relaxed in his chair, looking up at her. Only two things about him had changed: his brown eyes had narrowed and taken on a flinty stare, and his voice was steely hard. 'On trade matters between us and South America your expertise is essential to me, but the meeting in Sutton between me and Der Broeck concerns trade between us and the EU. You have little inside knowledge of that, therefore you would be unable to contribute to it anything of the slightest value.'

'You insult me!' White-faced, she gave him back stare for stare, her lithe body tensed as if it longed for the order to attack.

'That was not my intention and you know it.'

For a moment longer, Elena stood defiant, fighting for self-control. Then she swung away, returned to her place on the sofa and turned an arrogant glare on Danielle. 'Pour me another drink,' she ordered.

'Allow me, *madame*.' Gutierrez was in action in a flash. Fetching her glass he mixed her a fresh *pisco*-sour with a practised hand, then brought it to her and offered it gracefully. 'I hope you will find it to your liking,' he said, his olive-skinned, Levantine-handsome face smooth with solicitude.

She gestured for him to put the glass down on her table. As he did so she hissed some gutter-obscenity at him in Spanish. Her words struck the young Colombian like a blow, his hand jerked convulsively and he almost spilled the *pisco*. Swiftly recovering his poise, he set the drink down with great care then gave her a small, formal bow. '*Gracias, señora*,' he said.

Alvar had seen, and heard. 'We will leave you now, Elena,' he said coldly, getting to his feet and making for the door. 'Telephone me on your return to London. . . . I will take my pre-dinner walk now. Danielle, you will accompany me, please. I have points to clarify with you concerning the Sutton meeting.'

Danielle had been surprised by Alvar's instruction to join him, for he preferred to take his daily walks alone, and made no secret of it. In her room, as she changed into low-heeled shoes and slipped on a lightweight jacket, she decided he'd probably done it to annoy Elena. For a moment, she wondered what Carlos Fuentes had been like, and if Elena had loved him. . . . Alvar was waiting for her outside the Meridien's front entrance, and they set off together along the lit, busy street, past the lavish window displays of the area's upmarket shops.

'We will go round the perimeter of the park,' he said in his fluent, unaccented but often pedantic English, setting a brisk pace, limber in his impeccably tailored shantung suit. 'It will be more tranquil.' A few steps further on, they took a left turn and entered a different, quieter world. The roads were still broad, but as they walked them, the tall, elegant housefronts on their right were opposed only by the darkening green loom of the parkland lying unlit to their left.

'She is extremely jealous of you, you know,' Alvar said. 'Of the high favour I have shown you, and your consequent rapid advance into our inner circle. . . . Also, her jealousy of you has a sexual element. Elena has a sophisticated, carefully tended beauty; whereas much of yours lies in the bone structure of your head and face, and in your eyes.' He glanced at her sidelong and smiled. 'Besides, you are fifteen years younger than she is,' he added.

Danielle had been gazing into the shadowy reaches of the park, but as he finished speaking she turned to him. 'I don't think it's jealousy, I think it's plain, bedrock dislike,' she said.

'Which, equally plainly, is entirely mutual.'

She laughed and turned away. 'She is so clever at languages and the intricacies of the business, yet sometimes so blind about people,' she said after a moment. 'It's extraordinary, how she's never realized you and Ramon Gutierrez are lovers.'

'Or that I am enjoyably bisexual. It amuses me to see her so unaware. . . . You know, it is not only these jealousies she feels towards you, Danielle. Also, she does not trust you.'

'You think so? But, what *reason* can she possibly have?'

Suddenly intensely alert, Danielle was thinking, by God, if Elena does have the slightest factual cause to mistrust me I must find out what it is and deal with it, or I could be in deepest shit!

Fractionally, her voice had sharpened. Alvar glanced at her in surprise and saw her frowning. 'You have no need to be worried,' he said. '*I* trust you, and that is all that matters.'

'Yes. Yes, of course, and I thank you for it. I'd still like to know, though.'

'It is not a thing of reasons; it is of the emotions, and it is tied in with the jealousies. Elena does not like . . . she does not *want* you with us; she resents you being "one of us". She will not acknowledge that I depend on your skills and organizational flair. She would prefer things back the way they were before I brought you in and made you conversant with our confidential affairs: just herself, me and Ramon.'

Masking her relief, Danielle took up this point; she was surely safe enough there. 'Ramon is no real threat to Elena in the power stakes within the organization; she knows that, we all do. And with you she has a degree of pull because of the twin sons she had by Carlos. They're devoted to her—'

'And I to them, as she well knows,' he broke in. 'Do you realize, they are nearly nineteen now? Next year I shall bring them into the business. They are bright boys and ready for it. I am looking forward with much pleasure to seeing them next month, when we go to Argentina.'

Stealing a sidelong glance at him, Danielle saw a smile ghosting his lips, clearly he was lost in contemplating the bright future ahead. And his voice while he'd been speaking of those two blood-relatives of his had been soft and rich. Rich with sentiment, she thought. Sentiment and . . . sentimentality? Perhaps. The sentiment, the good stuff, the kernel; sentimentality, the outer shell – but God, I fear this man! Him, I do truly *fear*. Have done since I went under cover at the start of this job over two years ago. But that doesn't mean I'm afraid of what he might do to me, if— Perhaps I should be, but I'm not. I went into this with my eyes open, and for good reasons. Essentially, I volunteered. It's been a long two years, that's all. Nearly over now, thank God. After the Sutton strike I'll take me the holiday of a lifetime; I'll surely have earned it. . . .

'Danielle, you've realized who Johnson actually is, have you not? At Bristol?' Alvar asked.

'How d'you mean? Is there something special about him?'

'He is the man on whose account you came to my notice while you were working for Ryan, the supplier I employed in Cardiff. The man you helped to evade capture during that police bust two and a half years ago. After that episode we provided him with a new identity and a CV to go with it, then infiltrated him into Customs at Bristol Airport. He is not particularly senior himself, but he has suborned men who are. You did us a great service that night.'

'It hasn't done me much good with Elena, though, has it?'

'Nothing would.' Then Alvar's voice took on a sly inquisitiveness. 'Why does her enmity towards you alarm you so much?' he asked.

Alerted by his change of tone, she produced a small and mocking laugh. 'It doesn't *alarm* me! Why should it?' she temporized.

'Only you could know that,' he answered, smiling at her suddenly. Then both of them fell silent as a couple approached them along the pavement. As soon as the strangers had passed, Danielle steered the conversation away from herself and Elena. 'You had some details on the Sutton meeting you wanted to discuss, I think?'

'Indeed yes. Are the travel arrangements in order?'

'All complete, but I must let Mr and Mrs de Soto know Elena won't be coming with us. Late that Friday afternoon – three weeks ahead, we're talking of – I drive you down to Langley Manor. It can take over an hour as you know. Mr Der Broeck arrives there that evening, the discussions with him take place all through Saturday, then providing all's gone well, the contracts agreed upon will be signed on Sunday morning. He'll not be staying after that; his flight out of Heathrow's scheduled for around midday. You and I stay overnight Sunday and return to London on Monday. Have you decided what time you want to leave then?'

'There is no need for us to make it early. The main point of my staying on is to have all the Sunday afternoon to myself so I can enjoy the wonderful walk on the hills across from the Manor. . . . Good, all is well, then. Now I must tell you of a recent development which you must include in the documents you will be preparing for my meeting with Der Broeck. Two new supply routes are to be opened up. . . .'

Then, as they walked on together, the evening air warm about them, dusk shrouding the trees and shrubberies on their left into a place of mystery, Alvar gave Danielle Fraser a detailed resumé of the consortium's planned expansion into the countries of Eastern Europe, including data on the recruitment of personnel to facilitate implementation of the project.

Much of what he told her was confirmation and setting-in-context of names, facts and figures with which she was already familiar. But there was also a considerable amount of information that was new to her, and this she committed to memory. As well as enabling her to prepare the documents Alvar would need for his meeting, they would fill in some of the blanks in her own by now fairly comprehensive picture of Alvar's organization and its activities. Alvar himself was not aware of how nearly complete that picture now was, for she had taken care to conceal from him the fact that, in his absence, she was in the habit of plundering his computer-stored records without his knowledge.

2

Once well clear of the motorway out of London, Shearer settled back in his Volvo and gave himself up to the pleasures of driving a fine car through beautiful and, in this case, loved and familiar countryside. It was Sunday morning, and he was on his way to pay a flying visit to his mother at her home Glaslyn, some twenty-four miles north-west of the city of Hereford. Having rung Jack Curtis as soon as he got back from Spain and arranged to meet him in two days' time, he had left his PA in charge at head office and set off to see Natalie.

It was a pleasant day in early summer and he enjoyed the drive through this rich, red-earth heartland of England. When he had passed through Hereford and the town of Kington and was on the last few miles of his journey, his thoughts turned to his mother and the place which had been her home for the last thirty-odd years. Glaslyn: her ten-acre property in the Wye Valley, lying alongside the northerly bank of the river and sloping gently to the water. A good half of it was broadleaf woodland, but surrounding the grey stone house spread the 'garden' as Natalie called it.

Damn big garden, thought Shearer, smiling a little as he drove. For Glaslyn's garden was a full four acres of cultivated land supporting the apple and plum trees, vegetables, soft-fruit plants and bushes from whose harvest she and her band of workers produced the home-made jams, jellies, pickles and chutneys she sold in bulk to shops and hotels – including Shearer's own two hotels in Britain, one in Hereford, the other in Torquay. Honey and honeycomb also. Thinking of the honey, Shearer sighed to himself. The bees were his mother's special interest and he was remembering the times when she'd tried to make him share her fascination with them and their esoteric and highly organized life-style. Finally she had acknowledged and accepted failure: her son, her only child, loved the honey but remained indifferent to bees. He would never don veil and hat and enter with her into their complicated and wonderfully mysterious world.

Fourteen years now since Dad died: unbidden, the thought came into his mind as he turned off the road into Glaslyn's winding drive, and for a few moments the black memories flooded into his head. When, at the age of seventeen, he had refused to go into his father's prosperous travel and hotel business, had held out for entry into the police force instead, his father had closed his heart and mind against him. He hadn't disowned him: there'd simply been the one, tremendous, terrifying row between them, after which his father had gone cold on him and stayed that way until he died. That had been hardest of all on Natalie, who loved them both.

As Shearer rounded the curve of the drive and saw the house in front of him, the destructive memories of that furious quarrel died an instant death. The lived-into-the-stone peace of Glaslyn claimed him for itself; it always did. Originally built as a farmhouse, it had been added to and altered by successive owners and was now a large and rambling place. Its main entrance was at the side: thirty yards short of it the drive forked, the left turn leading up to the front door, that on the right to the courtyard at the rear of the house and on beyond to the business end of the property to give access to the gardens, orchards, storehouses, and two large kitchens.

Shearer took the right turn and pulled up in the courtyard. His mother had heard the car coming and, as he got out, she came hurrying through the back door to greet him, her black-and-white collie-cross dog Bart racing ahead of her. A woman of medium height, wirily built, straight-backed and workmanlike in jeans and dark-red fisherman's smock, her thick grey hair coiled into a French pleat at the back of her head, she greeted him, as usual, as casually as though he had been away five minutes. But as she walked into the house at his side her dark eyes were alight with pleasure.

'What a nice surprise!' she said.

'It's good being able to drop in unannounced.'

'That's one of the advantages of my life being so highly organized, people know exactly where I'll be when they want me.' She laughed. 'Sometimes, with some people, I wish they didn't.'

In the big kitchen, the central table was laid for lunch for one, and on the Aga opposite the back door, a casserole steamed gently.

'Smells good,' he said. 'Enough for two?'

'You can fill up on cheese.' Natalie was setting a second place at the table, putting plates to warm. 'Charlie Woodforde came up for a couple of days, brought me one of those splendid Stiltons he breeds. How's Clare?'

'I haven't rung her since I got back from Spain, too busy. Besides, I thought you would have, so I could catch up on her news from you.'

'She's your daughter—'

'And nearly twenty-eight years of age.' Shearer opened the grip he had brought in with him, hefted out a large carton wrapped in brown paper and put it down on the dresser. 'For you,' he said. 'Personal delivery from Barcelona. Can you guess what it is?'

'Easy.' Natalie put down the cheeseboard she had fetched from the larder and smiled at him. 'Easy, and thank you. It's a half-dozen bottles of Marques de Riscal, our favourite when we're in Spain together.'

'Which isn't nearly often enough. You should take more holidays.'

Now she laughed outright. 'Here's better than anywhere to me, you should know that by now,' she said, lifting the casserole off the Aga and putting it on the table. 'Come and sit down, I'm starving.'

Except during peak periods of summer and autumn harvesting and production, Sundays were rest days for Glaslyn's staff; and much as Natalie loved her work she always looked forward to and enjoyed having the day to herself. Now as she and her son ate lunch together she asked him about his trip to Spain where he was in the process of buying a partnership in a hotel on the outskirts of Barcelona.

'I'll be going over again in six weeks' time,' he told her, 'should finalize the deal then. But tell me how things are here. That's what I came for.' He gave her one of those rare smiles of his that she thought of as his 'proper' smile, as opposed to his 'social' one. While both softened the severe lines of his face, his proper one alone reached into his grey eyes and, briefly, dispelled the guarded quality usual to them. 'And to see you, of course,' he added.

Their eyes locked for a moment, and communed; to both of them it was like a close embrace. Then she said, 'I know,' and went on to bring him up to date with what was happening on the property and in the lives of the people who worked it, for, with the exception of the field and market managers, Natalie's fifteen employees were part-time, men and women from two nearby villages. And since Hal Shearer had spent most of his childhood at Glaslyn, and his daughter Clare had lived there under Natalie's care from the age of four, both he and Clare had known 'Natalie's people' for a large part of their lives.

Natalie did not ask her son about his private life, knowing him as a man fiercely defensive of his 'self'. For years now she hadn't asked. He'd been only twenty-one when, against his parents' advice, he married. Too young, she'd always thought; neither he nor his lover had been ready for marriage. She had been proved right. The girl had soon tired of it; her husband worked long hours and he didn't earn nearly enough to please her; the unplanned baby had been the last straw, and four years later she'd taken off. Since then, Hal had neither sought nor given any lasting commitment to man-to-woman love, Natalie knew. The half-dozen relationships he'd had over the years since then had all been ones in which rules had been drawn up and agreed upon in advance by both parties, the most important of them being that there was no permanent tie of any sort. As soon as either wanted out, that was to be unquestioningly accepted by the other. This choice of her son was a matter of deep sadness to Natalie; and even now he was in his late forties she had not completely given up hope that he might change.

That Sunday, sitting watching Hal clear their plates and the casserole from the table, Natalie thought, he's a fine-looking man, my son. Not so much handsome – too stern a face for that, with its strong bones, its cool eyes beneath those straight, dark brows – as intriguing. He has, I think, the aura of a man who's got a great deal out of life yet senses that something absolutely vital has escaped him somehow – and yearns for that *something*, is subconsciously searching for it. A certain kind of woman might intuit that longing in him, mightn't she? The sort of woman he might actually—

'Charlie's, or the Cheddar? he asked, passing her the cheese-board.

'Neither, thanks, or I'll never make it up the hill this afternoon.

Help yourself. Charlie must've thought I'd be having a dozen to dinner. I'll make coffee. When we've finished I want to show you the new hives. . . .'

It was four o'clock when they said their farewells and Natalie set out on her customary Sunday afternoon hike. Standing at the top of the five stone steps leading from the paved area at the front of the house down on to the lawn, Shearer watched her cross the freshly mown grass and head for the bridge across the river running along the valley floor, Bart, as always, close at her side until told he could run free. She had changed into walking shoes and knotted an ecru silk square round her neck, and had with her the shepherd's crook she'd come upon in one of the derelict outhouses when she and her husband first moved into Glaslyn. It was of yew wood, and its staff was carved with twining wild roses surmounted with the initials W.R.R.; but although she had prodded local memories for many years no one had been able to tell her the names the initials stood for.

As his mother and the dog crossed the bridge, Shearer looked away, stood taking into himself the wild and lonely beauty of the hills rising opposite the house. The land across there belonged to his mother's nearest neighbours and close friends, the Wilsons, whose family had farmed it for the last ninety years. Their house lay on that side of the water, two miles away and hidden from his view among folds of the hills. About half a mile up from the river and running parallel to it, their farm road slashed across the slope of the grazing land, an unsurfaced, tractor-wide track cut into reddish-yellow clay soil. He knew the route Natalie would take now; she never varied her Sunday walk unless forced to it by inclement weather. Once across the bridge she'd go up the zigzag track to that road then on along it, away from the Wilsons' farm.

His eyes returned to his mother and he saw her striding up across the cropped turf, heading for the road. She'd given Bart permission to roam and he was on the hunt for rabbits, streaming away from her, young black-and-white collie making for the nearest copse. Watching Natalie move up the sunlit hillside, Shearer knew she too was revelling in the feel, the time-rich essence of country, hills and sky. You're a brave and gifted and lovely woman, Mother-mine, he thought, and by God *I love you*. I know I don't show it much; but I know, also, that you're aware of it. Then he turned away, went round to the back of the house, got into his Volvo and drove back to London. Back to his other life – one certain part of which his mother knew nothing at all about.

Returning from Glaslyn to his flat in an apartment block near Heathrow, Shearer telephoned Jack Curtis and asked him to come over for a drink. Curtis had a house in Thornton Heath, a half-hour drive away for one familiar, as he was, with short-cuts between the two areas. He came over at once and they sat down in the sitting-room, whisky and soda to hand, and began talking over the present state of play in Shearer's targeting of Robert Alvar.

'Johnny Mack hasn't reported any change in Alvar's plans?' Shearer asked.

Curtis shook his head. 'Nothing of import. Only new thing is, he's not taking Elena Fuentes with him to the Sutton meeting.'

'Any particular significance in that?'

'None for you, that I can see. One thing's sure, though: Fuentes will be flaming mad about it. That can be dangerous to whoever she's mad at, with a woman so quick to fly off the handle.'

The two men had got to know each other when both were in the Force and, over the years since Shearer had 'been allowed to resign' from Special Branch in 1978, Curtis had become first his family friend and then, after a time, also his secret adviser in the personal vendetta Shearer became committed to, a one-man campaign against individuals in the top echelons of illegal drug-trafficking. And not only his adviser; also, his provider of relevant inside information. It was from Superintendent Curtis that Shearer received, clandestinely, the background knowledge on developments within the drug-running world given to the authorities by Mack, an ex-drug–runner turned informer. For although not himself an anti-narcotics officer – he worked in Communications and Liaison with the EU – Curtis had access to a certain amount of their data, particularly that relating to the domestic situation and business travels of their suspects. In the course of the last eight years, he had passed information on two drugs-trade supremos to Shearer in the clear knowledge of how it would be used, to what end it would lead if Shearer had his way; and when those two men had been shot dead he had felt no personal guilt in the matter, having come to believe that 'Shearer's way' was too useful, too effective where the law had failed to be properly so, for him to withdraw his support from it. Curtis had absolute confidence that in the event of Shearer being caught, he would divulge nothing of what lay between them; and although he was well aware that if it *did* happen then he himself would be bound to suffer by association with Shearer, he accepted that risk – largely because he considered his friend too skilled an operator ever to be nicked. Nevertheless, recently he had come to wonder whether the time had come for Shearer to call a halt to his one-man crusade.

' "Dangerous to whoever she's mad at".' Pensively, Shearer repeated Curtis's words, staring down at the glass cradled in his hands. 'Which in this case would be Alvar himself.'

Curtis smoothed back his thick, sandy hair, regarding his friend thoughtfully. His pale-brown eyes possessed a native cordiality which (as some had learned too late and to their cost) concealed a habit of shrewd observation and a hard-headed awareness of the possibility of man's duplicity. But the concern in them now was deeply felt.

'Make Alvar your last, Hal,' he said.

Shearer's head came up, his mouth hardened. 'Why?' he demanded. Then as Curtis stared back at him, silent, he gave a mocking laugh. 'What, you chickening out, Jack?' he scoffed.

But Curtis refused to rise to that. 'You've been lucky so far in all this, you know that,' he said. 'Those previous kills of yours, in the final analysis, police and criminals alike attributed them to internecine rivalries between various big wheels in the trade—'

'With excellent results from our point of view. Four villains were shot dead in the resulting little wars.'

'True enough. But luck can turn fast. And I've got a seriously bad feel about the Alvar hit, you gunning for him down at Langley Manor. Him, Fuentes, Gutierrez – they're a well-organized lot and not slow to spill blood. The thought of you on your own after *one of theirs* – it scares me, Hal. Don't know why it should, you've dealt with others much like them and gone scot free. But this one – to me it seems there's a different feel to it and I say to you again *it scares me.*'

Utter disbelief in him, Shearer bit back a sarcastic retort. 'Oh, come on now!' he said reasonably. 'I've had Alvar on my mind for the last year. I want the bastard dead, and this visit of his to Langley Manor offers the best chance I'm likely to get. The whole pack of them are off to Argentina next month, remember, and they don't plan on coming over here again till after Christmas. So forget it! You go on doing your part in this, pass Mack's stuff on to me. Leave the killing in my hands.'

Curtis accepted it; he had no choice. 'How's things with Clare?' he asked, to change the subject. 'Young Southgate must've been pretty pleased, her being assigned to your Hereford hotel to get more experience in Reception. She was telling me on the phone a couple of nights ago she hopes you'll let her try her wings at the Torquay place when she finishes in November.'

'I've got a surprise for her. Provided I clinch the Spanish deal, I want her to move over there. She's good, Jack.'

'You haven't done so badly yourself. And you started from scratch whereas she's had the advantage of your expertise and contacts. . . . Any signs of it developing into a serious thing, she and Southgate?'

'I don't know. It's good between them. That's natural, I suppose. Both of them only kids, no more than a year between them in age, and while she was growing up at Glaslyn, he was doing the same at Wye Grange not five miles away, their families good friends who shared the same country interests.'

'Big property the Grange. And his dad big money.'

'Didn't make any difference to the kids. Or their elders, come to that.'

Curtis drank some whisky. 'There was a time when I was cruelly jealous of Southgate,' he said. 'Seven years ago now. Long time.'

'I was aware of that.'

'Was I so obvious?'

'No. Natalie and I, we both knew you well by then. Still do, I'm glad to say; as you do us.'

For a moment Curtis was silent, staring down at his hands. Then he looked up. 'You should tell Natalie, you know,' he said.

'Tell her what?' It was a delaying tactic and as soon as he had said it Shearer despised himself for employing it, Jack surely deserved better from him.

'The killings, Hal.'

'I'll tell her when I'm ready.'

'Which is likely to be never.'

'Probably. But I'd like to dig a bit deeper into that point you brought up earlier,' he went on – anything to get Curtis off his back about telling Natalie. 'You said that for some reason you can't identify you've recently come to sense there's danger to me in my coming hit on Alvar. You said it *scares* you, and that's not a word you use easily. So, I'd like to toss the idea about a bit. Which of them is it sets your antennae quivering? Gutierrez, he's obviously a non-starter. So which? Alvar, or Fuentes?'

'Oh, Fuentes,' Curtis answered immediately, then grimaced and flung his hands wide in a gesture of surprise. 'That came out pat, didn't it? I wonder why?' he said. 'I've never tried to track down the feeling to one of the two before, yet out it came. Odd.'

'So let's consider Elena, the blonde and elegant Elena. In her early forties, widow of Carlos Fuentes, long-time drugs baron in South America, whose wife and partner in that business she became. Carlos was Alvar's well-beloved nephew, therefore after his death Elena was welcomed into the consortium and became Alvar's second-in-command. And that's all she is, Jack. What's in that to send you running scared?'

'If I knew, I'd either stop being scared or do something about it.'

'Maybe you should think back. Was there anything in the stuff Mack's been reporting about her that might be more important than you thought at the time?'

Curtis considered it, frowning, settling his compact body in his armchair, pressing his sleekly muscled shoulders back against its leather upholstery. What he was going to put forward was so tenuous that he didn't expect it to achieve much. Nevertheless he desperately wanted to get it across to Shearer.

Watching him, Shearer said to himself, by God I'm glad you've been with me in my vendetta, I'm glad you still are. And his mind went back to the last day he'd spent at 'the office', twenty years earlier. 'What's happening to you here, Hal, it's wrong,' Curtis had said to him then. Curtis was four years his junior and not long with the Met. 'I know I'm not the only one here thinking so, but stick with it, you should stick with it. Maybe later you'll come back to us.' Curtis had grinned then. 'Meanwhile I'll be your snout,' he'd said, joking of course. 'Keep you up to date with all that goes on around here. . . .'

But then, thought Shearer, as the years went by and Jack became my close friend, spent time at Glaslyn more and more often, became a fixture in its family life even when I wasn't there – then that joke of his became a reality, and helped me to bring into being my longed for other life which I couldn't tell even Natalie about.

'Elena Fuentes,' Curtis said, into the lengthening silence between them, 'is reputed to be an extremely vindictive woman. She's known to have pursued certain of her enemies to the death, quite literally *to the death*—'

'Nothing of importance to me in that,' Shearer interrupted, putting down his glass and leaning forward. 'The woman doesn't even know I, Hal Shearer, exist! The only way she could, would be if she'd found out about my vendetta, and she can't have.'

'Hear me out. Johnny Mack's info suggests Fuentes's revenges have been known to extend beyond the individual concerned.'

'To his confederates, you mean? Well, I'm in the clear there. I operate alone.'

'No, I *do not* mean his confederates! I mean *his family*.'

Shearer's face froze. 'But that's—'

'That's Señora Fuentes in action. In South America, granted, but it's only sense to admit the risk exists when she's in this country.'

'What are you saying exactly?'

'That there's Clare and Natalie to think of, not only yourself.' But in the face of Shearer's obvious scepticism Curtis had lost his sense of conviction. He shrugged and fell silent.

Shearer relaxed. 'You're out of your head,' he said. 'Clare in

Hereford, Natalie up in the sticks at Glaslyn – they're clear and away out of this, Jack. Except for you, *no one knows me for what I am.*' He finished his drink and stood up, holding out a hand for Curtis's empty glass. 'Same again?'

'Sure.' Then, as he watched Shearer pour fresh drinks, Curtis thought, strange things hunches. But as the evening wore on, memory of the one he had told Shearer about faded from his mind.

Having seen Curtis out that evening, Shearer poured himself a nightcap and sat down with it in the same armchair as before. It was his favourite, it had been in his possession for years. When Natalie had ordered its retirement from use at Glaslyn he had had it brought down to London and reupholstered: king-size, comfortably squashy and somewhat worn in places, it was a highly personal object in an otherwise smart, conventionally furnished room. As he sat down, the telephone on his side table rang. He picked up the receiver.

'Carver,' said the known, laconic voice.

'How did it go?' Carver was a long-time member of the criminal classes, and had been his snout during his last four years with the police. With weird but unshakeable loyalty, he had been on Shearer's side when the crash came. 'You ever want me to do a job for you when you're outa the Bill, you know, getting you inside info. an' that, I'm your man,' Carver had said then; and he'd meant it. Since then Shearer had made use of his varied talents on each of the three occasions he had set his sights on a target. And he knew him for a basically simple man entirely content to do the job asked of him while not taking part in the actual killing – both Shearer and Carver were well aware that that was the safest way for both of them. For some time now Carver had been working for him on the Alvar mission.

'No problem,' Carver said.

'No change of venue?'

'Nah. So I've done what you asked. Alvar'll be staying at Langley Manor. Mr and Mrs de Soto – his hosts I s'pose you'd call them if you didn't know what was really going on – they've been suspected of much in the past, never been brought to book, though. Alvar's been down there several times before; maybe those visits were straight, maybe not, I dunno. My two boys who sussed it out for me got an invite to a drinks do at the place as "friends of friends", ha, ha!' Carver's flat, faintly Cockney-accented monologue was punctuated by a brief cackle of laughter, then he resumed his report. 'I put up at a pub in Sutton, like you said. The Highwayman. Bloody good lot of blokes, in the bar there. Fond of a pint, too, 'specially if someone else pays for it. Aren't we all—'

'And happy to talk?'

'Very chatty. I've marked my mole, he's sort of houseman at the Manor, a temp. only. His girlfriend helps part-time there when they've got a shindig on. She came in the pub one night I was talking him up. Jeez, is she a looker—'

'Remember your age.' Rewarded for this effort with another snigger from Carver, Shearer returned the conversation to business. 'I've just learned that Alvar's taking only Danielle Fraser to the Manor that weekend. Fuentes has been told to stay home.'

'Hm. Will it make any difference to you?'

'I don't see how it can, just thought you should know. So get on now. Where's a good place for me to stay?'

'OK. I trawled through Sutton, and I reckon The Carlton will fit the bill. It's a medium-sized commercial hotel. Doesn't have its own car-park, but there's a large one nearby. You and your wheels will be able to come and go unremarked from both hotel and car-park.'

'Sounds good. Alvar goes down on Friday afternoon, his business is finished by Sunday. Der Broeck leaves that midday, but

Alvar and Fraser stay on overnight, leave on the Monday –
except that Alvar won't, will he? Right, then, you book me into
the Carlton from the Saturday through to the Monday. Do it in
good time. I'll need you to get me a car, but I'll ring you about
that closer to the day.'

'You want me to get you some maps?'

'No. Just send me those scale drawings of the layout of the
Manor and its surrounding countryside I asked you for. I'll be
looking the site over again before the hit.'

Ringing off then, Shearer reached for his glass and thought
things over. Everything appeared to be proceeding satisfactorily,
and soon he would receive Carver's maps of the planned killing-
ground. He looked forward to that with pleasure. They would
be meticulously correct in detail and skilfully executed, for
Carver was a trained and gifted draughtsman. Sadly, early on in
his career he had been suborned: other men had made use of
him, exploiting his talents to advance their own criminal enter-
prises. Four years in jail had drained him of ambition, but not of
his expertise or his delight in using it.

Carver, he's an artist *manqué*, Shearer thought, and he considered me a Special Branch policeman *manqué*. That's probably
why he's gone on working for me since I resigned from the
Force: he felt for me, he knew what it was like to lose out on your
dream. . . . The funny thing is, if Carver ever told me I ought to
walk away from what he helps me to do, ought to give it up,
shut it and all it stands for out of my life, then I'd give far more
consideration to *his* urgings than I do to Jack Curtis's. Strange.

3

Having signed off from her morning shift at the Reception desk, Clare Shearer went out through the front entrance of Greenways, her father's hotel in Hereford, and walked along the pavement, scanning the parked cars, looking for Mark Southgate's oatmeal-coloured Range Rover. Sitting behind the wheel, he saw her approaching, long-legged and fresh-complexioned, her mane of wheat-gold hair ruffled by the breeze, her supple, athletic body alive with vitality. His face lit up and he went to meet her. They were going to the races; his father had two horses running that afternoon.

'Are we all right for time?' she asked, as she fastened her seat-belt and he got in behind the wheel.

'Fine. None to waste, though.' He edged the car out into the traffic.

Clare smiled, happy to be with him. Mark was 'old' Mr Southgate's second son, but nevertheless he was going to inherit Wye Grange with its fine stables and wide acres because love of the land was in him, it had been born in him, bred into his blood and bone. The elder son had never had any heartfelt interest in the property and, after a civilized discussion with his father, he had gone into politics – to Mark's great good fortune, thought Clare now, and also to that of the estate.

'Natalie was over at the Grange yesterday,' Southgate went on after a moment. 'She came for lunch. Looked rather tired, I thought.'

'She works too hard. Seems to run in the family, my father's just as bad.'

There was a silence while he negotiated a busy roundabout, then, 'It's odd, Clare, but I still don't feel at ease with your father,' he said. 'Our families, we've all been friends since I was a kid, yet to me he's still basically a stranger. It's as if he's always holding something of himself back, as if there's a part of him he has no intention of letting anyone else know about.'

'He's difficult to get close to. Talia's always said it dates back to '78. You know, all the rotten things that happened to him then. It must have been a *horrible* year for him! His ex-wife – the mother I barely knew – she'd deen shot dead in Thailand in some seedy drugs-related shambles; I was just a kid, and no end of trouble to him, I've been told; then on top of all that came the police thing, him having to resign. His life was falling apart around him, he couldn't cope—'

'So Natalie took you up to Glaslyn to live with her.'

Clare chuckled. 'One of those "just until you get sorted out" arrangements that end up being permanent,' she said.

'Lucky me,' Southgate murmured. Then he asked, 'Does he open up to you? Really open up, I mean?'

'I've never been absolutely sure. I know what you mean about him. It's as if there's a part of his life he doesn't want me in – no, it's stronger than that, *he won't have me* in it!' But then, unnerved by what she had said, Clare pushed the subject away and took refuge on firmer ground, asking Southgate what time he would be leaving next day for the fortnight's conference he was to attend in Exeter. Being an official at it, he had to be there four days before it began.

'I'm making an early start, got a lunch date,' he answered.

'Really?' She turned to him, blue eyes glinting with laughter. 'Blonde, or brunette?'

But he would not play along with her banter. 'I wish you could've got time off and come down with me,' he said, a frown on his tanned regular-featured face.

'I *could* have,' she said crossly. 'Three or four days, anyway, which would have been fun. But as you know perfectly well, I didn't ask for it. I'm doing a job, and however unimportant that job may seem to you I'm not going to cheat on it, take time off just to enjoy myself.'

'Right. Sorry.' But then after a moment he slipped her a quick grin. 'And it *is* a woman I'm having lunch with tomorrow,' he said, 'but she's grey-haired, extremely sophisticated, formidably clever and articulate – also our chairman designate.'

In the stylishly appointed sitting-room of her fourth-floor apartment in Chelsea, Elena Fuentes mixed herself a rum sling at the bar cabinet alongside the large window overlooking the Thames and stood gazing thoughtfully across the river. Her mind was engaged with the enterprise she was about to embark on, providing matters developed the way she had reason to expect them to when – any moment now – Michael Larman, her nephew, came to see her. It was an enterprise slowly conceived over long years of bitter and vengeful memories; and now that the prospect of bringing it successfully to birth was close, her whole being was vibrant with tension. There was an element of sexuality in her excitement, she realized, and for a moment was consumed by a wild, lustful yearning for a past lost to her for ever. She controlled it, and sipped her drink. Out there beyond the spread of rooftops below her, the Thames flowed peacefully along between banks proud with the stalwart buildings of commerce and government. Elena loved that view. She never tired of it, for to her it epitomized her beloved England, the

England she had torn herself away from when she was twenty years old, running away from the desperate loneliness of life after—

The doorbell of her apartment rang. I pray God Michael will agree to do the thing I want him to do, she said to herself as she went to answer it. When I put the deal to him in outline three days ago it was obvious he was attracted by the amount of money on offer, and the checks I've had run on him show he's no stranger to risk-taking nor lacking know-how in the ways of lawbreaking and lawbreakers.

Mike Larman had known his aunt Elena for a long while. During his childhood she had several times stayed at his family home during visits to the UK, and then, as a teenager, he had spent three summer holidays on the Fuentes hacienda in Argentina. But since the death of his parents in a boating accident eight years ago, she had preserved a certain distance between them. He had picked up faint rumours of her involvement with Robert Alvar's drug-trafficking network, but in the course of his career as a freelance journalist he operated largely on the fringes of the criminal fraternity, and although he had many contacts on the inside of that separate world he was, to date, merely an observer of the activities going on within it. As such, he was not deeply trusted by its native inhabitants: his suspicions in regard to his aunt Elena had remained unsubstantiated.

As he followed Elena into her sitting-room, she waved a hand towards the bar cabinet and invited him to help himself to a drink, then sat down in one of the two velvet-upholstered armchairs placed facing each other across a low, rosewood table. Deciding on a beer, Larman poured himself a glass of Heineken. Sensing that she was regarding him intently, he took his time over it. He knew her for a clever, quick-tempered, experienced woman accustomed to getting her own way and not too choosy in the methods she used in achieving that goal and, while admiring her for that, he had come to her apartment determined not to let her bulldoze him into committing himself to a course of action on her behalf which he might regret later. However, he was attracted by what she had put on the table so far: he was to carry out for her a one-off job which would require his full-time attention over a period of around ten days. The pay-off was £50,000, half on his acceptance, the balance on successful conclusion. Sure, the job was outside the law; but his *own part* in it, Elena had assured him, would be only marginally and very briefly so. And—

'There's fifty thousand in it for you, Michael,' Elena said from behind him.

Christ, she's reading me like a book, he thought, and at once swung round and crossed the room towards her. 'I wish you'd call me Mike; everyone else does,' he said, sitting down in the armchair opposite her, seeing her face luminously resolute, the darkly blue eyes fixed on his, brilliant and calculating. When she looks like that she always reminds me of photographs I've seen of Eva Peron, he thought.

'That is why I do not.' Then she smiled at him and with it she became, he thought, beautiful and alluring. 'Looking at you always makes me wish at least one of my two boys had taken after your mother and me. They're both so like Carlos.'

Larman made no answer, he simply raised his glass to her and drank some lager. What she said was true, he knew, her two sons by Carlos Fuentes were by no means handsome, inheriting as they had their father's stolid, heavy-boned looks, his strong, stocky physique. Whereas he himself was a good-looking bloke, tall and fair, with broad shoulders, narrow hips, and the air of a guy who knew his way around. As he put down his glass he recalled how alike Elena and his mother, her older sister, had been.

'I never really understood why you went off to South America and married Fuentes,' he said. 'You and my mother, you must've had the men queuing up. I used to ask her, but she always just said you fell in love with him. I never believed her. Was it true?'

'No.'

'So, why?'

Elena stared at him for a moment, silent, and, he thought, curiously and most unusually defensive. Then her face stiffened and the blue eyes narrowed in an angry glare. 'You, the young. So insolent, so damned arrogant.' She flung the words at him then got to her feet, picked up her glass, went across to the bar and freshened her drink with neat rum.

Regarding her taut, angry-looking back, the luxuriant blonde hair swathed around the proudly poised head, Larman found himself, as always, attracted and intrigued by her. He was about to ask her the point of her last remark when she swung round and came to stand over him, glass in hand.

'And now we will talk about the manner in which an attractive, street-wise young man can find himself fifty thousand pounds richer in the space of ten days or so,' she said crisply. 'I gave you a rough idea of what I had in mind before I left for Spain, to give you time to think about it. On the telephone you said you were definitely interested. So now I will tell you what I want done.'

'I take it you'll pay any expenses I'll incur?' he enquired. 'I didn't bring it up before, but now we're getting down to the nitty-gritty it's something we'd better get straight.'

She searched his face, frowning a little. Then, 'Like mother, like son,' she murmured, and he thought he saw a glint of laughter in her eyes. 'Yes, your expenses will be on top of the fifty thousand.'

'Right. I've cleared my work sheet for the next fortnight,' he said, 'so go ahead. Brief me.'

Elena sat down once more in her armchair, sipped her drink then replaced the glass on the side table. 'You are to book into a certain hotel in the city of Hereford,' she began. 'There, you will make the acquaintance of one of the receptionists, a woman of twenty-seven.'

'Is she to act with me then? An accomplice?'

'Hardly. You simply make use of her to inform yourself on the nature of the terrain in which your operation will be carried out.' Elena smiled at him. 'You are an extremely handsome young man. You should find no difficulty in . . . gaining her attention, shall we say. Sufficiently to achieve your purpose.'

'Is *she* attractive?'

'Reports and the photographs I shall give you say so, yes.'

'Then isn't it likely there'll be a boyfriend around? I won't be able to—'

'There is one, yes, but he'll be away on business over the period of time we're talking about. That's partly why I've brought this hit forward, why I want it pulled off as soon as possible.'

Larman drained his glass. 'May I have another beer?' he asked, to give himself time to think. The terminology Elena was using had changed. This *hit*, she'd just said, and he didn't like it. Previously she'd referred to what she wanted him to do as a *job*. In the criminal world Larman prowled around the perimeter of, the connotations of the two words were poles apart. Therefore on his aunt's gracious 'Please, help yourself' he did so and ran his mind rapidly over pros and cons, only to discover that he didn't know of many bigger pros than £50,000 and all expenses paid. Nevertheless, he determined to press her later, to pin her down regarding the level of criminality in his own actions in this 'hit' of hers, should that fail to become clear to him as she unveiled her plans.

Elena had been watching him. 'It's easy money, Michael,' she said. 'And truly, what you have to do to get it holds few risks for you.'

'It's OK. I've decided: I'm in with you.' He went back to his chair and sat down. 'So go on – no, wait! Before you do, give names to the people and places which figure in this. It'll give me the feel of the set-up.'

She gave him a cold stare. 'Better not get too much *feel* in it,' she snapped. 'Don't fall for the girl!'

Surprised by the sudden change in her tone, he laughed it off. 'Have no fear,' he said. 'These days I'm suitably shock-proof that way.'

Shrugging away the split-second, sixth-sense unease which had needled into her, Elena relaxed and made a small smile. 'I'm sure you are. Well, the hotel is in Hereford and it's called Greenways. It's four-star. The woman's name is Clare Shearer. You are to make her acquaintance, wine and dine her, a show, whatever.'

'And what will I be looking to find out from her?'

'You are to get a detailed picture of the lie of the land at a property called Glaslyn which lies twenty-four miles from Hereford, about four miles beyond a town called Kington. Glaslyn belongs to Clare Shearer's grandmother; they're close, the girl visits frequently.'

'Why d'you want this detailed picture of the place?'

'I don't. *You* will, in order to make the hit.' Elena got to her feet and went across to the fireplace. Picking up a framed photograph from the mantelpiece she stood gazing down at it, her back to her nephew. He watched her for a moment, wondering without much interest what the photograph showed, then he drank again.

'This year I came back to the UK with two purposes in mind,' Elena said, breaking the quietness which had settled over the room. 'One was to consolidate my position within my uncle-in-law's import-export business over here.'

'And the other?' Sensing an extreme tenseness in her, Larman prompted her silence.

She turned to him. Her eyes were unfocused, she was not seeing him. And there was such a stillness about her that she seemed a figure carved from stone: a figure imbued with will, purpose – and malevolence. 'The other is revenge,' she said. 'Blood for blood.'

He found his voice. 'I won't be part of a killing.'

'I'm not asking you to be. You are concerned with the first part of the Glaslyn hit only.' Elena's mesmerizing stillness broke, she returned to her chair and sat down. 'Now, I will give you a general picture of the property,' she went on. 'It will be for you to use your acquaintanceship with Clare Shearer to acquire inside information about it and its people's way of life, their habits, so that you can make an informed choice as to the best time and place for you to carry out for me the first step of my scheme.'

Larman's eyes went down to Elena's hands spread-fingered on the arms of her chair. She had rather large hands, long-fingered, strong, immaculately manicured; and he saw that her nails were clawed deep into the grey velvet, showing darkly red, taloned. They look almost . . . *feral*, he thought, and for a moment was unsure of his commitment to her. But then his imagination created inside his head a picture of one of those hands signing a cheque for £50,000, and at once he recommitted himself.

'Who is it I'm after?' he asked.

'The woman's grandmother, her name's Natalie Shearer. Listen, now, here's what I wish you to do.'

4

Langley Manor lay in a long and lovely valley some six miles south of the town of Sutton, a rambling dwelling dating back to Tudor times. Some parts of it were built of grey stone, others of red brick, time-mellowed to a dusky rosiness. Situated 500 yards up from the valley bottom, it was surrounded by extensive landscaped gardens embellished with arbour and pergola, with lily pond and gazebo. A paved terrace ran the length of its frontage. From one corner of this, a gravelled path led down alongside the wide sweep of lawn in front of the house, on through the band of woodland covering the valley floor and the lower rises of the opposing slopes and then out on to the pastureland beyond where, through long-time lack of use, it had faded to become a barely discernible track.

All this Shearer observed through his binoculars when he made his second and final recce the next Friday afternoon. As before, he parked his hired car in a lay-by two miles short of the property, slung his glasses round his neck and took to the hills, working his way down to the valley bottom then up across the slopes the other side to a spot opposite the Manor where a wind-eroded knoll provided him with shelter. Hunkering down in the lee of this, he studied his hunting-ground long and carefully, committing to memory such facts about it as would be important to him on the day he went after Alvar.

When he was satisfied, he lowered his binoculars, relaxed against the sun-warmed slope at his back, half-closed his eyes and, awake, dreamed his dream. Quiet country, this, he thought. And nowadays, according to Carver's mole, that path down there is seldom used except by guests at the Manor who like to walk countryside. Which Robert Alvar does. So it's a near certainty that after Der Broeck has left – which he's scheduled to do before lunch that Sunday – Alvar will be out here in the afternoon. He'll take that path leading down from the house, intending to go through the woods and on into the open country beyond: he's bound to, from the house it's the only decent country walk on offer. . . . . There in those woods: that's where I'll take him.

At 6.30 that evening, Shearer telephoned Clare, knowing she would be off duty, and broached the possibility of her working at the hotel in Barcelona. The prospect delighted her, and they talked it over at length.

'That's great, then,' he said finally, 'I'll go ahead with it. How's life in Hereford?'

'Fine. I'm out for a film and supper in half an hour.'

'With Mark?'

She laughed. 'Hardly, he's down in Exeter. The environmental conference; he'll be away two weeks. I *told* you.'

'So you did. Who're you going with, then?'

'A guy named Mike Larman. He's staying at Greenways, a journalist.'

'Have I met him?' Clare's male acquaintances were many and Shearer had long ceased to maintain a fatherly eye on them.

'Not yet. You will, though. I like him, and I'm taking him out to Glaslyn next Tuesday, Talia's drinks do. You're coming up for it, you promised her, remember. Look, I must go now or I'll be late.'

'If this guy Larman's going to stay around he may as well get used to that.' Then, after an exchange of farewells, Shearer rang off. The name Mike Larman had already drifted out of his mind.

Robert Alvar maintained a *pied-à-terre* in London, an elegant, three-storey house in the St John's Wood area. It was governed by his cook-housekeeper, a Mrs Adams, a dark-skinned, angular woman devoted to his service ever since he had helped her only son to flee Britain and set up a night-club in Prague. On his return from Barcelona, Alvar had taken up residence there, for he had considerable business matters to attend to in London.

The day when Shearer telephoned his daughter and first heard the name Michael Larman had been a frustrating one for Alvar. When he finally got home at 7 p.m., being informed by Mrs Adams that Señora Fuentes was awaiting him in the sitting-room did not please him at all. But he put a brave face on it. Going on through from the hall he greeted Elena with the warmth and geniality he was so gifted at assuming and project-ing, then mixed her a *pisco* sour and poured a stiff whisky and water for himself. For a while they chatted amiably enough about the social side of her trip to Rome. Nevertheless, observ-ing her as she sat coolly *soignée* in the armchair beside his Bechstein, blonde head poised, the cut of her midnight-blue tussore two-piece complimentary to her shapely figure, Alvar sensed a tightly controlled tension in her. Intrigued, he sought to define it. He decided it was not powered by one single primary emotion alone, by love, or fear, or anger, et cetera. So was it, he wondered, born of a subtle mixture of several such deep-seated emotions and these perhaps in conflict with each other?

He did not like being uncertain about the reasons underlying Elena's mood. He had worked his way up to his position as kingpin of the consortium not only by several strategic killings and a myriad ongoing intimidations, but also, in many cases, by discovering and then using to his own advantage the desires and inmost feelings motivating the people he worked with (or, in his earlier days, *for*). Such knowledge, he had found, enabled him to manipulate individuals and to maintain his pre-eminence among his own. He had no intention of allowing Elena to escape him now.

'Leave that aside for the moment,' he interrupted as she railed against a colleague in Rome whom she suspected of lying to her. 'You are very angry, and I can tell it is about something a great deal more important than Emilio's possible duplicity. Tell me, what is troubling you, my dear? You know I will help if I can.'

She stared at him for a second then looked away, reaching for her glass. 'It's because of Sutton, the Manor,' she said. '*I* ought to be accompanying you, not Fraser.'

Alvar did not believe that was the reason for her present edginess. She had recovered her poise fast, he acknowledged that. But before she turned her head away her eyes had betrayed her, he had seen them flare with sudden alarm. She had got up her guard now, however; he was aware of that and smiled, knowing he had her on the defensive. And Elena was not good at defence; she excelled in attack alone.

'But Danielle does all my paperwork, I need her there,' he said.

'Der Broeck won't require many documents. Both you and he already know most of the relevant facts. He'll only want to talk money, and for the two of you to sign the contracts.'

'That's a ridiculous simplification of the situation between Der Broeck and I, and you know it.' Alvar got to his feet and went to stand in front of her, not close but near enough, he hoped, to force her to look up at him. But she would not do so, sat clasping her glass with both hands, staring down into it. 'There's more to this than you are telling me, Elena,' he said sharply. 'I want to know what it is.'

Sullenly, she gave him an answer. 'Fraser – I don't trust her.'

He turned his anger on her then, forgetting his intention to ferret out what lay at the heart of her present mood. *'You do not trust her?'* he repeated, his tone icy. 'She saved one of our men from that bloodbath two years ago and you say you do not *trust* her? *Nombre de Dios*, woman! Danielle proved herself that night, proved not only her courage but also her loyalty to us and ours!'

'And since then?' Elena, too, was on her feet, confronting him, blue eyes ablaze. 'What has she done since then? For us? Tell me! Go on, tell me one thing she's done for us that a hundred others of our people couldn't have done if you had given *them* the opportunities you've given her!'

'Are you questioning my judgement?' Alvar stood rock still and spoke quietly, but such was the menace coming out of him towards her that she stepped back a pace. Vivid remembrance of certain instances of the disciplinary action Alvar had visited upon men who had questioned his authority within the organization, rushed into her mind: such punishments had been swift, mind-blowingly painful and bloody, and when the resulting bodies had been returned to relatives they had needed nametags to establish identity.

'No,' Elena said and, with her head still high, turned away, walked to a glass display cabinet on the opposite side of the room and stared at the Persian miniatures arranged on its shelves.

Behind her, Alvar was smiling. He was entirely sure she was not seeing his exquisite treasures. In some ways he pitied her. Such a cold, hard woman. She had, he felt sure, never been truly in love with anyone in all her life. Certainly she had not deeply loved Carlos; she had married him largely for his money and for the 'in' it gave her into the power- and money-rich underworld of the big-time narcotics trade. Sad, to be forty-odd years old and never to have loved—

He dismissed all that with a shrug. Picking up her glass and his own he freshened both drinks then replaced hers on the table beside her chair. Sitting down again in his place he sipped his whisky and considered his next step. He had dismissed his anger with her, the point she had set at issue between them gave him no concern whatsoever. He had had a high opinion of Danielle Fraser's potential as long as three years ago, soon after she had been taken on strength by one of his lieutenants; and her rating with him had risen yet higher when she had brought off her rescue of the wounded Ted Evans during the fracas in question. That daring feat of hers had so impressed Alvar that shortly afterwards he had appointed her his own PA.

Since doing so he had never found cause to fault her or to doubt her absolute loyalty to himself, and he had no intention of demoting her in any way simply to placate Elena.

He decided to go back to his first objective: to find out the real reason for the tension in her. And he knew that the best way to get the truth out of Elena was to disorientate her a little and then – jump her.

'I apologize for my discourtesy towards you,' he said pleasantly, 'I reacted without thought. You just told me you do not trust Danielle, and I have a certain respect for your instinct in such matters. But I also am a good judge of people and *I do* trust her. Therefore, I need you to give me your factual reasons for suggesting that I am wrong in doing so.'

'Why is it she has so few friends? Just that one ancient aunt she visits from time to time – the rest, it's only letters.'

'That is not sufficient, Elena. The aunt, we have investigated fully; the letters I myself keep watch on.'

'Then why isn't there a lover around? She's attractive enough—'

'You know why. For five years before she came to us, Danielle worked in Australia. Her man there – she had gone out there to be with him – was killed, lost overboard in a yachting tragedy. So she returned to Britain. She has not forgotten that man. She loved him. Maybe one day she will love again, but not yet. It is a thing I admire in her, Elena.' He paused briefly, then said with cutting sarcasm, 'I should be grateful if you would now tell me your real reasons for distrusting her. All you have offered so far are mere . . . what is it? Decoys? No. Evasions. Yes, evasions. I will have the truth now, if you please.'

She sat down, drank some *pisco*, replaced her glass. Finally, 'I don't have anything definite against her,' she admitted. 'It's simply. . . .' Her voice trailed away and there was silence in the room.

Alvar waited, perceiving that as he did so, and as the silence grew longer, her defences against him were going down. As soon as he judged her sufficiently unguarded, he would strike. The oblique assault: in circumstances such as pertained at the moment that was his favoured approach for getting information out of anyone who had no intention of providing it.

Into the quietness between them, Elena said, 'Danielle knows too much. About the consortium and its network of suppliers and distributors. About me, you, Gutierrez. By now, every aspect of our organization is known to her. Whereas she . . . she seems so enigmatic sometimes. It's almost as if she knows something we don't. As if all the while we're conducting our affairs she's not only in there with us, assisting, but also a part of her is somehow *outside* us, is going about its own agenda and *is hostile to us.*'

'You are getting very imaginative, my dear.' He was mocking her.

'You think? Beware of her, Roberto, there's this feeling of secrecy about her—'

Alvar struck. 'And you, Elena?' he interrupted harshly. 'What about *you*? Are you always totally open with me?'

'*Me?*' She was on her feet, staring at him, her eyes wide with shock. 'What are you saying, what are you suggesting? I have no secrets from you!' she protested. 'I'm *always* honest with you—'

'You have always dealt honestly in the business, I grant you that. But the word I used was "open", which to my mind means nothing is hidden, *all* plans and *all* actions of either of us are clearly revealed to the other. So I ask you again, have you, since we came back to England and especially these last two months, always been totally *frank* with me?'

'Of course I have—'

'*No you have not!*' Then moving close to her, he made his accusation. 'You have been planning a little clandestine operation of your own, I believe,' he said, and watched contentedly as astonishment, uncertainty and anger gutted her face. She has never been able to lie to me convincingly, he thought, and what a boon that has been to me over the years. Then he saw fear surge into her eyes. It swept aside all other emotions and Alvar smiled inside himself, knowing he would get the truth from her now.

'All right,' Elena said. 'Yes, what you say is true . . . Roberto, please understand, there's something I must do, and I'm working on it, have been working on it without telling you.'

'What is it?'

'No! Please, no! It's entirely personal. It's absolutely nothing to do with the consortium, I swear!' She laid a hand on his arm. 'Let it go, Roberto,' she begged. 'Please, let it go now.'

Then suddenly he was her friend again. 'I believe you,' he said, taking her hand and kissing it, then turning away to sit down. 'But I still want to know what it is you are engaged in.'

Sullenly, Elena turned away. Picking up her *pisco* she stood sipping it, taking her time, making him wait a little longer. But she knew she would have to give in. Robert Alvar ruled with an iron hand. Turn him against her and not only would he ensure the swift destruction of the operation she was planning, which was so dear to her heart, but also, he would remove her from his protection and from her position within the consortium. *If nothing worse. . . .*

'May I pour you another drink?' he asked politely, as she put down her empty glass. He hadn't minded waiting; he knew he'd won.

She shook her head. 'What I'm planning to do is on account of my brother,' she said quietly, not turning round. 'It's about Jim.'

James Smith, brother to Helen Smith (now by marriage Elena Fuentes) and her sister Elizabeth. Alvar had not heard her speak of her dead brother for years, and had long since assumed she had at last let go of the memory of him and the manner of his death. Now, listening to her, he realized he had been wrong in that.

She sat down and faced him, ramrod straight, her eyes wide and filled with bitterness. 'Strange, isn't it?' she said. 'Just saying his name, it gives me pleasure.'

'He died twenty years ago,' Alvar said sharply, for there was a fey look about her that he did not like, it was not her style at all and seemed somehow to place her beyond his control, which was not to be tolerated.

'And the man who killed him has lived his life through every one of those twenty years Jim never had. Lucky man. But his luck is going to run out soon.' Looking into her eyes Alvar saw them brilliant with triumph – and the full implication of what she had just said dawned on him.

'You intend to put out a contract on the life of this man?' he demanded incredulously.

'Yes. But not immediately—'

'After all this time? You cannot mean it!'

Her mouth twisted. 'You don't understand, do you?' she said. 'All the years you've known me and you still haven't realized.'

'Realized what?'

She gave a slight shake of the head. 'It doesn't matter.' But she was thinking, no, you never would realize, and if you did, you wouldn't understand, would you, being you?

Suddenly impatient of it, Alvar returned to the matter of clarifying her intentions. 'You are being evasive. I want the truth of this. What did you mean by saying "not immediately"?'

Leaning her head back against the soft suede of her chair, Elena linked her hands behind her swathed blonde hair and smiled at him. 'I plan to make my brother's killer know what it's like *to suffer*,' she said. 'His death will come later, after he's paid to me in kind for the suffering he's caused me and mine.'

5

Clare had ridden the Longmarch Hills outside Hereford many times in her life, but this was the first time she had done so with Mike Larman at her side. Since he had arrived at Greenways a week earlier, she had been out with him several times, to meals and films, and to Natalie's drinks do at Glaslyn. At all those times they had spent together he had shown himself a charming, world-wise man, and fun to be with. To her he was a fresh face on the local scene; there was a certain élan about him, and she had been glad of his company. But that summer-sweet afternoon when she took him to the stables she herself used, and they rode out together into the countryside south of the city, she saw a side of him she had never guessed at.

He was obviously entirely at home with horses. That she realized within ten minutes of them riding out, for she saw a true, remembering joy in the lift of his head as they set their horses to the slope of the first hill and the light breeze quickened about their faces. As they rode on into the open country, he on a dapple grey, she on a roan mare, they did not talk much; nevertheless, by the time they stopped for a breather forty minutes later, the relationship between them had undergone a subtle change. On Clare's side this change was little more than an extension of her interest in him, and of the ease and pleasure she found in his company, but for Larman it was something deeper; he was beginning to feel that a bond of intimacy was spinning itself into being between himself and the young woman riding at his side (only later was he to recognize that he fell a little in love with Clare Shearer that afternoon on the Longmarch Hills).

Reaching the crest of a long rise they dismounted and turned their horses loose to graze. Sitting down side by side on the cropped turf with their backs to the sun, they stretched out their legs in front of them, pulled off their hard hats and gazed out over the countryside spread below them, a green and pleasant land basking in the sunshine showering down upon it out of a cloudless sky.

'Look, you can just pick out the cathedral.' Clare pointed towards the city islanded amidst fields and woods. But Larman did not answer, and when she turned to him she saw he had tilted back his head and closed his eyes. Sunlight caught his fair hair and sharpened the contours of his tanned and handsome face, giving it a harshness she had not perceived before. Suddenly chilled and uncertain, she looked away. I don't know what it is he's thinking about, she thought, but I do know that at this moment he's not really here in the hills, he's in some tougher and more vicious world.

As though he had sensed her withdrawal he opened his eyes and looked at her even as she was turning away from him. 'You're a fine horsewoman, you know,' he said. He wanted to get her back with him and it was the first thing that came into his head.

'Yes, I do know,' she answered, a kind of sadness in her. Then she banished that feeling as idiotic and faced him again, smiling. 'And do *you* know something? You're a far better one. It was born in you; me, I was taught. Sure, I learned well but it's not the same thing.'

Larman drew up his legs and circled his arms around his knees. 'I first got on a horse in Argentina, when I was a kid,' he said, brooding on the green fields below him. 'That's what I was thinking about just now. I haven't ridden for years, and coming out here like this brought it all back. My aunt married there, her husband had a ranch and my mother and I used to visit for holidays. Grasslands to dream about, there.' He grinned. 'The horses seemed to feel that way, too.'

'Tell me.'

And at once he began to do so, reliving the memories as a starved man eats. Yet after a few minutes he stopped abruptly, throwing up his hands, turning to her with a dismissive, 'Hell, you don't want to hear all this. And anyway I was only a kid, I don't remember it that well.' But his last words were a lie. He remembered the exotic and brilliantly exciting splendour of Elena's hacienda vividly. But as he spoke, it had been Elena herself who'd dominated his memories – then with terrifying suddenness she'd leapt out of memory straight into his present consciousness, blonde and arrogant and ordering, 'Play the girl discreetly, Michael. Keep your personal background out of it.'

The grey lifted his head and shook his trailing reins, began to move away. Glad of the distraction, Larman whistled softly to him; the horse pricked an ear to the call, quietened, settled to graze again.

'How's life and business at Glaslyn?' Larman turned back to Clare. Then, as she happily reported on Natalie, the dog Bart and the various activities in progress at the property, he warned himself to keep his tracks well covered with this woman, talking to her a moment ago he'd come close to being too loose-mouthed concerning his family connections, particularly his aunt Elena. Long-legged and lovely as Clare was, she was *of the enemy camp*; he must keep that in mind at all times and preserve a certain distance from her. But as they sat so companionably close, their backs to the faint breeze and the afternoon sunlit about them, he realized that doing so was not going to come easily to him, especially after he had completed his part in the operation against Natalie Shearer. Elena's instructions had been clear: he was to do the job; he was to ensure that he had an unbreakable alibi covering the period of time involved in doing it; and, after it was completed, his relationship with the girl was to continue for a few days exactly as it had been before, Clare Shearer must not perceive any change in him. Then, in his own time, he was to fade from her life.

As they rode on together that afternoon, Mike Larman had indeed acknowledged to himself that he was going to find it difficult to live out the necessary lie to Clare through the remaining days of his stay at Greenways. But the prospect of £50,000 deposited in his bank account again stiffened his resolve to do so.

Curtis's house in Thornton Heath was a place of modest size set in its own half-acre of land. A little after seven o'clock on Thursday evening, as he was settling down on his veranda to enjoy a beer and a look at the paper, his doorbell rang. To his surprise it was Shearer. He invited him in, collected another can of beer and a glass from the kitchen, and they went out on to the veranda together.

'Did you come over for anything special?' he asked, as he sat down again.

'No.' Shearer strolled across to the veranda rail, leaned both elbows on it and studied lawns and flower-beds. 'Your roses need dead-heading and the grass could use attention,' he observed.

Behind him, Curtis grinned. 'I like it the way it is. You, you're a purist. Do everything by the book.'

'Ha! Really? You can't say that about my "sideline" work! And that, as you well know, has always been the job I most care about.'

Curtis frowned. 'It's gone on long enough, Hal. Way I see things, it's best to stop while you're still winning.'

Shearer drank lager then turned and leaned back against the rail. 'I can't, Jack. *It needs doing.* The ways drug-trafficking's being opposed legally – they simply aren't working! You know that as well as I do. Oh sure, they're keeping the lid on, just about, in the UK at least. But not for much longer, in my opinion. Look it in the eye, man! The world's being flooded with addictive drugs. Illegal trading in them's corrupting whole rafts of the social, economic and political life of the Americas, the Middle East, Asia – and we certainly aren't succeeding in controlling its entry into Europe. Just look at Britain! On the personal level we've got drug-related tragedies on a huge scale, and as for nationally – Christ! Think of the vast sums spent on attempts at rehab. – then think of all the other things that cash could be spent on!' He slammed his open palms hard down against the rail at his back, pushed his rangy body upright. 'A guy's got *to do* something! You look around you, you listen, you read and – hell, you've got *to do* something! Well, I damn well have.' He gave a wry smile and added more quietly, 'With your help, the information you pass on to me.'

Curtis did not want to talk about it. 'It's your life, Hal,' he murmured, telling himself he was a coward, and changed the subject. 'All's well with Natalie?' he asked.

'She's fine, very busy as usual.' But Shearer was not so easily distracted from what he wanted to talk about. Sitting down in the cane chair alongside Curtis's, he put his glass down on the floor. 'Ten days from now and I'll add Alvar to my tally,' he went on. 'I hope this one doesn't turn out a dud like in Barcelona.'

'That was a spur-of-the-moment job. This one's long-planned.'

'It's looking promising, but I can't plan for him too, can I? Sure, I've been building towards taking Alvar out, amassing info. on his personal life as well as his business affairs. I know his habits as far as an outsider can, and "one good walk a day" is one of them. Still, occasionally he doesn't do it – and one of those occasions could be *that* Sunday. He could stay in, or someone might go with him – that's very unlikely, though, he likes to go by himself, especially if he's out in the country. . . . The way I work, I can never be sure till I've pressed the trigger. That's the downside of it. The upside is I'm always ready to fold my one-man tent and steal away; and always ready to start at the beginning again.'

Curtis finished his beer and stood up, empty glass in hand. 'What type of weapon did Carver get for you this time?' he asked, eyeing Shearer's bent head sombrely.

'Walther .38. Silenced, obviously.'

'And you'll dispose of it yourself afterwards?'

'As always.'

'You need any help?'

'None.'

Curtis waited, hoping for more, for some sharing of the details of Shearer's plans for the hit. It did not come. 'These operations of mine, Jack, I thank you for your help in them; but when it comes to the killing, that is mine alone.' Shearer had said that to him a few days before the first of his strikes, ten years back. And it had been the same each time since then.

'Ready for another drink?' he asked after a moment.

Shearer looked up and nodded. 'Thanks,' he said; and lifted his glass in a silent salute, drained it, then passed it up to the waiting hand. 'Whisky, please.'

That same evening, despatched by Alvar to sit in for him at a meeting of potential clients, drug dealers, Danielle rang the bell of The Haven, a detached bungalow near Streatham Common in south London. She was admitted by a matronly middle-aged woman, and led into the front room. This was furnished like an office, and at the centrally placed table, three men sat awaiting her arrival, two of them whites in their thirties, the third a Colombian and much older. He, clearly the senior, rose and saw her seated with them, then opened what developed into a somewhat confrontational conference. Being there merely as an observer representing Alvar, Danielle took no part in the discussion. She listened, and noted down key facts and figures. However, as she did so, she was also observing the body language and facial expressions of the three in what was clearly not a meeting of minds. That was what Alvar had sent her there to do. 'Act like a simple stenographer,' he'd said, 'but assess for me the private rivalries between the three.'

After the meeting had broken up and she had made her way out into the hall, one of the younger men followed her and invited her to have dinner with him. She declined. His face tight with anger, he went back into the sitting-room. Danielle smiled and let herself out of the front door: she had other fish to fry before returning to Alvar's house in St John's Wood.

Slender and lithe in her grey business suit, shoulder-length dark hair swinging free, she walked to the shopping area of Streatham High Road, as always making sure she was not being followed. Arriving at the post office she found an unoccupied telephone booth in the row of four outside it and placed her call. It was expected – she had sent him a coded message two days earlier – and on the second ring she heard the receiver lifted at the other end of the line.

'Oberon,' she said.

'Calling who?'

'Caliban.'

'You've got him,' he said. And hearing the tautness go out of his voice she imagined him lying back in his chair and putting one hand up behind his head – or more likely he was stretched out on the futon in his bedsit on the second floor of the rooming-house in Tottenham, he was a lazy dog when not engaged in hands-on action. Caliban: it was she who had suggested his *nom de guerre* for the mission, he was so damn rugged good-looking it simply had to be sent up somehow. This was the first time they had worked together; and it had gone, was going, well. As soon as Alvar had told her she was to accompany him to Langley Manor for his meeting with Der Broeck she had contacted Caliban and put him in the picture: it was exactly the sort of opportunity they, together with many others, had been working and hoping for. Caliban would ensure that all necessary prepa-rations were put into place, ready for the springing of the trap that – hopefully – would eventually see Alvar and his associates behind bars.

'His plans are basically unchanged,' she told Caliban now, 'but we might travel down later than I told you. That's likely to be immaterial, but it's best you know.'

'You think I might throw the panic lever if you don't show up there on the dot?'

At the mockery in his voice, a clear picture of his face came inside her head: his dark, straight hair thick and probably uncombed, the squarish, stubborn chin, his eyes and the well-formed mouth doubtless amused. . . . She did not give his ques-tion the dignity of answering it. 'There's something I want you to do if you possibly can,' she said.

'Name it.'

'Can you bug Elena Fuentes's phone?'

'Bug La Señora's phone?' His voice ridiculed both the sugges-tion and her for making it. 'Christ, no! Not a chance – unless it's essential to the success of our operation? One slip and they'd be alerted, the entire op. would blow up in our faces!'

'I can't say it's essential. OK. Leave it.'

'You sound uptight about this. What's up? Why Elena?'

He was disturbed, she sensed it and instantly wondered whether, in fact, her own apprehension was justified. It certainly was not rooted in factual evidence.

'These last few days, she's been . . . different. It's as if she's excited about something. But there's nothing coming up in the consortium's affairs to warrant that, nothing really big scheduled for the near future.'

'What sort of excited? Anger, fear, love—'

'None of those. It's difficult to put a label on it.' Danielle paused, recalling and examining the nature of the feeling she had intuited in Elena Fuentes. After a moment she identified one possible interpretation of it and, as she did so, was aware of a small and sickly fear stirring to life deep inside herself. 'It's as if she's gloating over something she knows is going to happen,' she went on slowly, 'maybe something *she's* going to cause to happen—' She broke off, gave a short, nervous laugh. 'Shit, no, forget it.'

'No, we won't. Are you sure it's nothing to do with the consortium's affairs?'

'I don't see how it can be. I know all that, and there's nothing, like I said.'

'So it has to be some personal scam or whatever. Or' – she heard his voice go cold and hard and knew he had thought of the same possibility as had occurred to her a few seconds earlier – 'or *she's on to you!* Dan, could *that* be it?' he demanded, then at once went on to reason that appalling possibility away. 'But if it was, she'd have told Alvar—'

'And I'd probably be dead by now. Yes. But she's a very devious lady and she doesn't like me one bit, so we can't rule it out. Could be she's playing cat-and-mouse with me, she'd enjoy that. Don't let's forget, though, it could be some other ploy altogether, some personal coup she's close to bringing off.'

'I'll have the boys run another check on her. Anything else?'

Good, Caliban is back on even keel again, Danielle thought. But for a moment back there he'd been worried out of his head for her, she could tell that, and for a second the lambency natural to her amber eyes flared yet more strongly: the knowledge was one small, friendly spark of light in the otherwise dark and lonely world she had to inhabit while working undercover against the Alvar organization.

'That's all,' she said, thinking, not much longer now, thank God.

'You take care, now. Fuentes is one scheming and ruthless woman, and she's loaded with cash. In my experience all that can be a dangerous combination.'

6

The following Saturday afternoon, Natalie had a telephone call from Clare. Sitting on the window seat in the living-room she chatted with her granddaughter for several minutes, telling her about the affairs of Glaslyn and its workpeople. Then she asked, 'How's Mark? He's been on the phone, I expect?'

'He rang yesterday. It seems the conference is proving more than a bit dull.' She laughed. 'He says things pick up in the evenings, though.'

'Don't you mind?'

'All those West Country beauties, you mean? Heavens, no! He's—'

'He's in love with you, has been ever since you were teenagers, and . . . well, you're so *right* together—'

'Hey, if you go on like that I'll start calling you "Grannie"!'

It was teasingly said but Natalie caught an edge to her voice. 'Well, I am one, so although I wouldn't like it I couldn't quarrel with it, could I?' she said equably. 'Nevertheless, I'd rather you didn't.'

Clare laughed. 'Anyway, I didn't ring you to talk about Mark. I wanted to know if you'd mind if I brought Mike Larman out to Glaslyn next Tuesday? It's my day off. I told him it was jam-making time and he said he'd love to see how it's done. "The production line", he called it, which made me giggle a bit, but he's really interested. Besides, he's invited us for lunch at The Woodcutter's Arms afterwards.'

'Who suggested The Woodcutter's, you or him?' The pub was Clare's favourite, and famed locally for its game pies and venison.

'Me. Will it be all right? You remember Mike? At your drinks—'

'Of course I do. Tall, fair-haired, handsome and charming. Very articulate. I liked him. He and Bart took to each other, too, I remember.' And indeed, Natalie recalled, he'd certainly added to the liveliness of her party. 'Are you going out with him tonight?' she asked.

'No. Sadly, he's had to go to Leominster. He left early this morning. I'm standing in for Maria all evening, on Reception. How about you? Are you socializing this weekend?'

'No, thank goodness. There's a dinner over at Wye Grange; I was going but I've called off, too tired, it's been a busy week.'

'Sunday tomorrow, you'll have the whole day to yourself, be on top of the world again by Monday.'

'Sunday indeed! Lovely thought. I'll laze over breakfast, put in some piano practice, then in the afternoon me and Bart'll take off—'

'Over on the hill, along the Wilsons' farm road and Bart chasing rabbits real or imaginary.' In the staff rest-room at Greenways, Clare smiled. 'Don't you ever get tired of that walk? Want a change?' she asked.

'Never. Too beautiful.'

At 1.30 the next day, Sunday, as arranged earlier between them, Mike Larman rendezvoused with Skinner at the White Hart pub on the outskirts of Hereford. Wearing a well-used Barbour jacket, a black baseball cap on his fair hair, he ordered a gin and tonic at the bar. While it was being poured, he looked over the clientele. As expected, Skinner was sitting at a small table tucked away in the furthest corner, a half-full tankard of beer in front of him. Larman paid for his drink, then picked up his glass and joined him.

'The draught beer here's ace,' Skinner remarked, a slight grin curling his long, thin mouth.

'You've got all the gear?'

'Sure have. The gun was a bit of a teaser – not much call for that sort. Got it OK in the end, though. The whole shebang's out in the Land Rover, under the groundsheet.'

As they finished their drinks they did not talk much. Their plans were already well rehearsed, the White Hart was simply their agreed starting point. Larman took stock again of the accomplice he had hired. Skinner was barely thirty, with a narrow, bony face and mousy hair; his knowing, pale-blue eyes gave the impression of being as old as time itself. According to his reputation, he possessed all the requisites for the job he'd been hired for. He was wiry of body, tough, and experienced in the use (and acquisition) of all sorts of firearms. And, importantly, not only was he happily wedded to a life of crime but also the word within the criminal underworld was that once bought, he stayed bought; he'd never been known to grass on an employer since the beginning of his career sixteen years earlier. On letting it be known among his contacts within that separate and esoteric world that he had a job for a hitman, Larman had stressed the importance of that last factor, for he'd observed at first hand how easy it could be to suborn yet further those already bent to one man's purpose. During the preparations for that Sunday afternoon's operation the man had proved his worth, obtaining all the equipment needed for it and showing a quick grasp of the scheme Larman had devised.

'Ready?' Larman asked, as Skinner put down his empty

tankard. He nodded, and the two men got up and made their way out.

Skinner had parked the Land Rover on the far side of the car-park. Unbuttoned khaki anorak loose about his lean torso, belted blue jeans low on his hips, he led the way across to it, got in behind the wheel and started up the engine. Larman climbed in beside him and they drove off, heading towards the town of Kington twenty miles away. The afternoon was warm, the sky was blue, and on both sides of the road the rich, rolling country of middle England smiled back at the sun. Conversation between the two men was minimal, and what there was came in short bursts. Larman sat relaxed, enjoying the view. Skinner concentrated on his driving, his big hands surprisingly dextrous on the wheel.

'You've come up with a good vehicle here,' Larman remarked after a while. 'She looks the part.'

Skinner smiled his closed, lopsided smile. 'About fourteen years old, looks like she's been used hard and taken a few knocks, and there's plenty of new mud on the old to show she's an active work-horse. Must be a thousand like her around both here and where we're going, folk ain't gonna give her a second look.'

'The number plate could do with a clean.'

'True.' He chuckled. 'Not so mucky for the fuzz to pull us off the road, but it sure ain't easy to take in fast. Not that it matters much, straight after this job she's going in for a total revamp.' He grinned. 'Useful, friends are. 'Specially ones who own garages.'

Later, as they were driving along the Kington bypass, he asked, 'Who's behind you in this ploy?' Then he shook his head and phrased the question differently. 'Shit, you're not going to tell me that, are you? What I was wondering is, what's this old lady done to deserve what's going to happen to her?'

'None of your business. Lay off it.'

Clear of Kington now, Skinner said no more. Nevertheless, he did not stop wondering. The strange nature of some of his jobs, the weirdness and complication of many of his clients' outside-the-law actions and motives, fascinated him. Forbidden detailed knowledge of them in most cases, he wove stories of his own about them – and, just occasionally, had later found his imaginings revealed as truth in the national Press, sometimes accompanied by financial information about his paymasters which caused him to wish he had charged them a lot more.

Soon, then, Larman leaned forward in his seat as they rounded a bend. 'A hundred yards on, there's a turn-off to the left,' he said. 'We take it and go on across the river, on to a farm track across the hills.'

Skinner drove the Land Rover off the highway and across the bridge over the water. There, tarmac gave way to a broad dirt track that cut back into the hills for a short distance then struck off to the right across the slopes, running roughly parallel to the river. Soon they sighted a substantial, grey stone farmhouse off to their left, behind the curve of the hill they were traversing. Larman pointed to it.

'That's Wilson's farm,' he said. 'It's a couple of miles from where we'll be operating, but we'll be well out of sight of it. They're not running any sheep this way at present so no one'll be around checking stock. I'll tell you when to park. There's a passing-place to the left of this track, surrounded by trees. That's where we leave the Land Rover. Make sure she's well under cover.'

Skinner followed instructions. When he had switched off, both men got out and went to the back of the vehicle. There Skinner halted, stood looking about him, breathing deeply, stretching. 'Nice day for it,' he observed. 'Our hide's two hundred yards on from here according to your sketch map.'

'It is.' Larman unfastened the tailgate, then threw back the tarpaulin.

'You tote the gun and ammo,' he said. 'I'll bring the ground-sheet.'

'You're the boss.' Grinning amiably, Skinner reached in and lifted out the special rifle; then, side by side, they set off along the dirt road towards the place Larman had selected for their ambush. As they left the shade of the trees masking their Land Rover, sunlight flooded over them and they saw the grand sweep of the hills spreading out in front of them, running down to the river flowing along the bottom of the valley. Then they came to another copse, this one growing on the left side of the track only, running close alongside it, bushes and tangled undergrowth massed between the trunks of the trees. There, Larman called a halt.

'This is it,' he said, and turned and forced his way through greenery into the copse.

Skinner stood still a moment longer, cradling the gun, examining the scene with a professional eye. In front of him, partly forested hillside sloped down to the river where, almost dead opposite him, a slat bridge straddled the water. A hundred yards or so up the slope rising the other side of it stood a fine stone house surrounded by extensive orchards and gardens. From a paved area at the front of the building a gravelled path led down to the bridge then, on his side of the river, continued, a rough trail now, ascending in gentle zigzags to the road on which he was standing, reaching it a dozen or so yards beyond him. Turning on his heel, he studied the copse Larman had entered: it edged the tractor-wide road thickly, low-growing hazels and undergrowth crowding in among the grey trunks of tall ash trees. Skinner smiled: cover would be no problem. Nor would the action: the old lady would come down out of the house to the river, cross the bridge and walk up the path to the road. Whether she then turned left or right to walk along it wouldn't matter, he'd step out into the open and—

'OK, you reckon?' Larman had rejoined him.

'It'll be a dolly. Where've you stashed the groundsheet?'

Larman jerked his head towards the trees behind him, 'Under a rowan with a scarred trunk.'

'Then you and me'll get hid up, lie doggo till she shows.'

'She usually sets out around four. An hour to go.'

But they did not have to wait that long. Crouched at Larman's side behind the screening bushes and undergrowth edging the Wilsons' farm road, Skinner spotted Natalie twenty minutes later as she came down across the lawn, heading for the river.

'We're on, I think,' he muttered.

Larman raised his binoculars, pushed them through the hazel leaves in front of his face, leaned forward and focused them on the figure now crossing the bridge, dog at heel. 'We're on,' he confirmed after a moment.

'Brilliant!' crowed Skinner softly. He eased his loaded weapon into position, poking the barrel out through leaf cover. Sighting along it, he tracked his imaginary target first right, then left along the road in front of them. Then he drew the gun back. 'She won't feel a thing,' he said.

Straightening up, the two men watched Natalie come up the hill towards them, following the trace of the grassy, zigzag path. It did not take her near any of the stands of trees dotted across the pastureland so they did not lose sight of her. As she drew nearer, Skinner saw the dog with her race off suddenly, black-and-white streak of energy heading for the nearest trees. He laughed.

'Off rabbiting,' he said. 'What make is it?'

'Collie-cross.' Larman lifted his binoculars to his eyes again. He could see Natalie clearly now, a slim, straight-backed woman in beige trousers and dark-green overblouse, a rose-red scarf covering the hair he knew to be grey. Her shepherd's crook in her right hand, she came up the sun-bright hillside clearly loving every minute of it, her step vigorous and a lively eagerness about her. Centring the glasses on her face, he saw a small, closed smile lengthen her mouth—

'Shit,' he said softly, and turned away, shoving the binoculars back into his pocket.

'What's with you?' Skinner glanced round at him curiously.

'Nothing. You ready?'

Skinner smirked. 'Me, *I've* never been *un*ready.'

Larman glared at him, then forced a quick grin. 'OK, then, bully for you. Now let's get on with it,' he whispered. 'Remember, if the dog susses us out, leave it to me. I'll handle him.'

Skinner nodded, then looked back down the hill. 'We better shut up. The dog's near on.'

Padding up onto the farm road ahead of Natalie, Bart immediately caught a scent and loped off along the rutted track, nose to ground as he followed it.

Larman had been holding his breath. Now he let it out. 'Gone away from us, good-oh,' he murmured.

Skinner was busy with the gun. Whichever way the dog went the woman would go too, he reckoned, and he was checking his field of fire accordingly, squinting along the barrel until he was satisfied. 'Right, then,' he muttered. 'Come on, lady, let's have you.'

Stepping up on to the farm road, Natalie stood still for a moment, crook in hand, looking back the way she had come. Then she set off after Bart, who was snuffling into a burrow at the roadside.

Skinner centred the gunsight on her left shoulder-blade. 'Got you,' he breathed, and squeezed the trigger.

Struck fair and square, Natalie gasped in shock, looked round wildly and, half-turning as she fell, pitched forward to lie sprawled on the road, her crook trapped beneath her body, her rose-red headscarf glowing brilliant against the reddish-yellow earth.

At the burrow ahead of her, Bart's head lifted sharply as she fell. Instantly sensing disaster, he dashed back to her. Whining, he nuzzled her shoulder, licked her face – then suddenly intuiting human approach he raised his head and crouched beside his mistress, pale eyes fey, teeth bared in a snarl. But the man coming closer held out his hand towards him, friend-talking him as he did so. 'Bart,' he said, 'good dog, good fellow. Come, Bart. All's well. Come.'

Tail down, the dog slunk towards him, belly-low to the ground, not yet quite sure of him. He examined the offered fingers with his nose. He explored the cadences of the man's steady voice as, softly, confidently, it spun its mean web of deceit about him. And then after a little while he licked the hand of the man who had been a guest at Natalie Shearer's home.

7

At 5.20, Mrs Wilson was picking sweet peas in the garden at the side of her house when suddenly the sun-drenched tranquillity of the afternoon was shattered by a racket of barking from the yard at the back. Calling to her three farm dogs by name, she hurried to investigate, hearing the row quieten as she went. By the time she reached the yard all was peace: with much tail-wagging all round, Towser, Floss and Ben were mobbing Bart, the four had been friends since he was a pup. Puzzled by the arrival of Natalie's dog alone and out of the blue, she called him to her. There was a two-foot long piece of rope hanging from his collar. On examining it she found its loose end had been chewed through. Gripped by a sudden apprehension, she hurried into the house and telephoned Glaslyn.

A gipsy-dark, vivacious woman of thirty, tailored jeans and a scarlet blouse setting off her sturdy body, Eve Wilson tapped her fingers impatiently on the windowsill as the phone rang and rang unanswered at the other end of the line. Finally she hung up, and considered what to do next. Her alarm increased as she recalled that Natalie had been on the phone to her that morning, saying how glad she was it was Sunday, how lovely it would be out on the hill with Bart that afternoon. Ten minutes later Eve was in the family's Range Rover heading for Glaslyn, her trusted-neighbour key to its back door in her pocket, Bart nervy and watchful on the seat beside her. She found Natalie's Fiesta parked in the back yard, but when she went through the house, calling – with Bart at her heels, whining, pawing her legs whenever she stood still – she found no one there.

Going outside again she relocked the back door and leaned against it, arms hanging loose at her sides, thinking. Bart was growing more and more agitated, leaping up and down at her, clawing her legs. Then, suddenly, he licked her hand, closed his mouth carefully upon it and pulled, his eyes fixed on hers, a soft growl deep in his throat.

'What, Bart?' She bent down and stroked his head. 'What do you want, fella?' Then it came to her: Natalie's walk on the hill! Bart had been with her of course, and now he was saying *get over there!* Something's wrong, you slow-witted idiot human – *do something about it!*

Eve set off at once. Dashed down across the lawn at the front of the house, over the bridge and on up the track leading to the farm road, Bart at her side. Fear was driving her now, for her imagination was creating various horrible scenarios to account for Bart being loose with a gnawed-through rope round his neck. Natalie never tied him up. But someone had, that afternoon – *and what appalling reason could anyone have for doing that?*

Coming from low in the western sky, sunlight slanted in along the valley giving every stand of trees on the hillside its own elongated patch of shadow. The hill lay entranced in a lovely serenity. Only the woman and the dog moved upon it, an urgency in them, both dreading what lay ahead of them, the woman because she did not know what they would discover, the dog because he did.

As they drew close to the farm road, Bart suddenly gave a low whine, left Eve's side and raced on up the track. She saw him turn to the right when he reached the road. She saw him slink along it, head hanging, tail between his legs – then suddenly he sat down, lifted his nose to the sky and threw one long, moaning howl at the blueness above him. The lament keened through the sunlit air. Eve's mouth went dry, her scalp crawled. '*Natalie,*' she cried, and pelted on up the rest of the slope, stumbling as she reached the road, peering along it right, then left—

But there was no Natalie-shape lying on the rutted earth there. Eve could see only a black-and-white dog sitting in the middle of the road, silent now, his muzzle still pointed at the empty blue heavens. As she began to walk towards him he stretched his body out on the ground and laid his head between his paws. It was not until she was close to him that she saw what it was he was keeping guard over. Shielded by his body lay Natalie's carved crook; and beside it a pool of blood stained the yellow-brown soil of the hill.

8

'I can't believe nothing else was found at the scene yesterday. Just the crook and – blood.' Shearer's voice betrayed no emotion, but exhaustion and mental strain ravaged his face, his cheeks were drawn, his grey eyes red-rimmed and anguished.

The man's in a torment of fear for his mother, thought Police Inspector Dwyer, studying him. Then he considered further, frowned, and essayed a deeper analysis of Shearer's present mind-set: he's afraid for her, yes, but I suspect there may be more to it than that. I've got a feeling there's *a sense of guilt* in him.

'Hopefully this morning's search will give us something more to work on.' The inspector sat back in his chair. 'We didn't have a great deal of time. Mrs Wilson rang Kington at 6.32 and they had men on scene within twenty minutes; but it was another hour before our Hereford men got there.'

'I know it.' Shearer swung away impatiently, crossed to the window and stood looking out. They were in the sitting-room of the private penthouse flat on the top floor of Greenways – comprising in addition two *en suite* bedrooms, kitchen and bathroom – and it offered a panoramic view across the city. But Shearer was seeing none of it. 'Glaslyn, the grounds, the hillside – everywhere was searched for evidence,' he went on. 'Blood sample, photos of recent tyre tracks on the Wilsons' farm road, near and not-so-near neighbours questioned – oh, you did a fine job, no question. But not much came of it, did it?'

'Analysis of the blood and the tyre tracks will be at the station this morning. I've told them to phone me here if anything comes in before I get back.'

Shearer turned to face him. 'What I can't see is, why they removed the body.'

'Hang on.' Dwyer heaved his bulky frame out of his armchair and crossed the room. 'We don't know she's dead,' he said.

'What else can I think? That she's being held for ransom?' Shearer threw up his hands in disbelief, his mouth bitter. 'Christ, if that's the idea behind this, whoever's got her must be out of their heads! There's fifty or more families round here they might get more out of than us!'

Dwyer kept to his own point. 'Right from the start it's been pretty clear that Mrs Shearer herself doesn't have any enemies in the sort of league we're probably dealing with here,' he said. 'So last night I asked you if you knew of anyone likely to be nursing a grudge against you, a serious grudge. You said you didn't. But that was then: you knew only a few facts and they gave you the horrors, and in addition you'd been driving for four hours to get here. You're rested a bit now, so I'm asking you again: can you think of any enemy of yours who might conceivably be doing this? Might seek to strike at you, through her?'

Shearer brushed past him and sat down in the chair the inspector had been using. 'I may be rested, but the answer's the same. It's no.'

Too pat? Dwyer wondered. A mite too definite, perhaps, for a man who's made a good deal of money in what can be a fairly cut-throat business when you're up amongst the big boys?

'Oh I'm not denying I've made business enemies over the years,' Shearer went on. 'I have. But none of them are the sort we've got to reckon with in this.' Then he changed the subject. 'If only your men could find the weapon we'd have something to work on,' he said. 'Was it a hand gun, d'you think—' He broke off as the telephone rang.

Dwyer took the call. He identified himself, instructed his caller to go ahead, then stood listening intently, interrupting once or twice with a question. Catching the drift of the conversation, Shearer realized he was receiving a report on the analysis of the blood found on the hillside.

'Let her not be dead, just *let her not be dead*,' he muttered, and controlled his private demons of terror and guilt as best he could.

'Lab. reports,' Dwyer said as he replaced the handset.

'What do they give us?'

'Some cause for hope, maybe. The blood is her type, yes, but it comes from superficial wounds only.'

'You mean she's alive?'

'I can't say that, and you know it. I mean that she received superficial cuts, probably from a knife.'

'Which leaves us where we were before.'

'Not quite. Whoever did this knew what they were doing. They simply wanted a fair amount of blood left on the scene. Which to me suggests abduction. If they'd wanted to kill her they could have.'

'You mean the blood was left there to prove they had her?'

'Quite likely. They'd know it would be analysed.'

'Dear God.' Shearer dropped his head, whispering the words. Then abruptly he looked up again, glared at Dwyer. 'But if she's been abducted, why hasn't there been a ransom demand?' he asked aggressively.

'Take it easy. Keep your mind focused on the pluses we have. As to what they do next, remember this took place barely twenty hours ago and most of that was night time.' The inspector turned away and headed for the door. 'I'll get back to the station,' he said. 'The reports on the tyre tracks should be in any time now.

If that Land Rover sighting we got from Kington ties in with what shows up there, we may have a lead.' He halted at the door, looked back at Shearer. 'If you do get a ransom demand you'll let us know at once, won't you?' he said. Then, getting no answer, seeing the eyes in the harrowed face turn steely hard, '*Don't*, Mr Shearer,' he warned. 'People have tried to sort out this kind of thing on their own before, you know. It seldom works.'

'A ransom demand – should I expect one soon? If that's the object of this?'

Dwyer did not answer immediately. He stood thinking it over, his face expressionless. Finally he said, 'It's impossible to tell. I'd have thought it'd come soon if it's coming at all. But I've known cases where the abductor plays his victim like an angler plays his fish. He might leave you on a loose line for a bit, or he might promise you a date for a hand-over and then not honour it. He might play it any way that occurs to his vicious mind. Ones like that are either psychos, or they harbour some deep-seated hatred towards their victim.' He held Shearer's eyes. 'Play straight with us in this, Mr Shearer,' he said levelly. 'If this is an abduction, and whoever's holding your mother is that last sort I spoke of, we're into a fearsome game. That kind, they're bastards. Bastards,' he repeated, then turned and went out of the room.

Clare had finally got to bed at 3 a.m. the previous night, tired out mentally and physically by the horrible events at Glaslyn and, later, by the emotional impact of her father's arrival at Greenways. But life had to go on, and she was at work by nine o'clock the next morning. Nevertheless when her coffee break came up she decided to break with habit and take it in her bedsit in the annexe rather than in the staff rest-room. The moment she closed the door behind her she let out a huge sigh of relief at being out of the public eye, slipped off her high-heeled shoes and padded across to the narrow melamine counter running along the wall opposite. The small stainless steel sink set into this was flanked by a work-surface on which stood an electric kettle, a tin of biscuits, various mugs and the necessities for making tea and coffee.

She made herself a mug of coffee then stood in her stockinged feet, cradling it between her hands, considering what to do next, if anything, bar drink her coffee. Mike Larman ... should she phone him? Several times during the previous night she had fervently wished she could call him, ask him to come and help out with all that was going on; but she'd known that was impossible, he'd said he wouldn't be back from Leominster until the small hours, that the meeting he was attending would be 'a boozy affair'. Well, she decided, as she dialled his room number, he should have slept it off by now.

'Hello, Mike,' she said when he picked up the phone. 'Have you heard?'

'Yes. They told me at the desk when I came in last night, must have been around two o'clock and, to be honest, well, I wasn't good for much but to fall into bed. I've been wondering whether to ring, but thought it better to leave it to you. Clare, I'm so sorry. How can I help?'

She managed a light touch. 'Are you sober?'

'I was from the moment I got the news, actually, but they said you were tied up with the police. Where do things stand now?'

'No big leads so far. I've been on the phone to the Glaslyn staff and various friends. Eve Wilson's looking after Bart, the Parrs are dealing with house and garden stuff, and Jean Prentice is keeping the business side running smoothly – she's been Talia's right-hand woman as long as I can remember, so there's no problem there. I'm about to drive over to see how things are, help out if I can. Will you come, Mike? I'd really love to have you with me if you've got the time.'

For a few excruciating moments Larman felt torn in two. His

head said, don't go with her! Don't spend time with her now; it could be dangerous to you; make your excuses, then get right away from here soon, clear out for good. His heart didn't say much, but the words it did say were words of power and he found himself unable to withstand them.

'Give me ten minutes then I'll meet you at the desk,' he said to her, 'I'll make a couple of phonecalls, then I'll be free for the day.'

During the drive out to Glaslyn, Clare told him about her father's arrival at Greenways in the small hours of the previous night, of his emotional devastation, his helpless fury.

'That's what really gets you,' she went on. 'There's this anger screaming inside you but *you yourself* can't do anything about it. It's out of your hands and all you can do is – wait, bloody wait!'

Sitting beside her, Larman looked at her and was appalled. He knew he'd got in too deep with her, but knowing it wasn't making things any easier for him. He had told himself it would be easy to walk away from her after the job was done, but now he saw she was hurting, he did not want to walk away.

'I feel for you in this,' he said, hesitantly. 'You were so fond of her—'

'*Fond of her?*' Tight with anger, her voice slashed across his and he broke off. She pulled the Honda in to the side of the road and switched off. Sitting straight and stiff, she stared ahead of her along the empty road. 'There's something I'd like you to understand,' she said coldly. 'It's this. I'm not bloody *fond of* Talia. I *love her*. I love her right in here.' She laid her clenched fists against her breast then lowered them into her lap. 'She's been mother and father to me. My real mother ran out on us when I was a kid, and my father – yes, he's splendid, I do love him, but I've never been able to get really close to him. I've tried, but at some point along the line he always puts the barriers down. . . . But Talia, Talia I love close, closer than anyone in my whole life.' She turned and stared him in the eye. 'Do you understand what I'm talking about, Mike? Have you ever really loved anyone?'

After a moment he looked away from her. 'No,' he said. 'No, I haven't.' And he knew at that moment that he would walk away from Clare Shearer. He had to. He would stay awhile and help her in anyway he could, but then he would return to his own way of life £50,000 the richer and with no lasting regrets for what he had done. Otherwise——. 'I'm sorry,' he said, dismissing a sadness which had crept into his vitals at his momentary perception of the depths of his own loneliness. 'Let's get on now, there must be a lot to do at Glaslyn.'

As they drove on he asked, 'How's your father taking this? I can't imagine him giving way to his feelings. Such a battened-down sort of guy. I know I've only met him the once, at the Glaslyn drinks do, but talking with him . . . well, those grey eyes of his seem to be holding you at bay all the time.'

'He has good reason to be that way. More than most, anyway.'

'Really?' Glancing at her he saw her profiled face as resolute as her father's and, intrigued, he enquired further. 'How come?'

'It all happened twenty years ago. Most men, probably, would have shrugged it off after a bit. My father never has. He's not the kind of man who could, perhaps. He needed to put up defences at that time, and he's never dismantled them.'

'What happened?'

Clare hesitated a moment, then decided to give him . . . a little. Not everything, though, because although he was an understanding sort of bloke and was helping her now, he was after all an outsider and as such was not entitled to knowledge of sensitive family matters.

'He was in the police,' she said. 'Anti-narcotics operations, he was a trained marksman. One time, he screwed up a police bust and he was forced to resign. He and quite a few others considered that an injustice, too draconian by half. That didn't get him anywhere, though. He was out.'

'But he's made a good life for himself since, hasn't he? The hotels, it must be very interesting, very satisfying. Besides, he's not exactly poor, is he?'

'True. Talia staked him and he built a new career, heads a thriving business now. But . . . you see, to him working against drug-traffickers wasn't simply a job, it was a, a mission. Talia says he had a gut-hatred of them and their trade. Me, I suspect it's never left him, and that *because he can't do anything about it* there's a lot of frustration and resentment in him, and that's why he holds back from people on a personal level, it's to . . . well, I think he still hurts inside and doesn't want anyone to know it.'

Larman nodded. 'Could be. Waste of a good man, though, wasn't it, him leaving the police? Everybody's loss.'

Clare drove on for a good half-mile in silence. Then she gave him a quick smile. 'Thank you for that, Mike,' she said, and a few minutes later turned off the main road and drove down to Glaslyn.

9

In Natalie's absence there were many things to be attended to at Glaslyn, and Clare and Larman drove out there again the following morning. But Clare was scheduled for duty at Greenways at three o'clock, so they started back straight after lunch.

'House, garden, business – it all seems to be running like clockwork,' Larman observed, as Glaslyn fell away behind them.

'People round here, they're like that when a neighbour has problems. Most of them, anyway.' Then, having brooded on the phrase he had just used, she added, ' "Running like clockwork": good way of putting it. Clever you.'

'How d'you mean?'

'Clockwork: efficient performance, but no living heart to it.'

He changed the subject. At Glaslyn Clare had had a long telephone conversation with her father, so now Larman asked how he was.

'It's hell for him, pure hell.' On the steering wheel her hands were white-knuckled. 'Not knowing where she is, or even whether she's alive or dead. Shit, what kind of people are these, Mike?' she went on. 'What is it they want? If it had been a random crime, some maniac striking out to kill whoever's unlucky enough to be nearest – well, surely he'd have left the body where it lay? There must be more to it than that. But, what? Who? Talia, me, my father: I'm not saying everyone loves us, but

I just can't imagine any of us having enemies who'd operate in the sort of league we seem to be dealing with here!'

This is dangerous ground for me, thought Larman; and asked if the police had given them any more information. She told him the authorities were working on the assumption that Natalie, alive or dead, had been removed from the crime scene in a Land Rover. That widespread vehicle checks were being carried out on the strength of the tyre tracks found near the scene. That three local people had given descriptions of Land Rovers they had seen at times and places which might, or might not, have significance. That it was suspected two males had been involved in the attack—

'Anything particular about the two blokes?' Larman interrupted. 'Any details that might help in identifying them?'

'None. There's no definite leads at all,' Clare answered. And when he sat back, silent, staring out through the windscreen, she thought how glad she was he was there beside her to talk things through. 'It's good, having you with me, Mike,' she said. 'You'll be staying on a bit longer at Greenways like you said, I hope?'

'Of course. I've finished the local research I came up to do; I'm my own boss, I'll simply get on with collating it here instead of going back to London to do it.' He did not want to stay. He wanted to get the hell out and away from her, for in her company his guilt in the affair troubled him. But he had realized that to leave now, as he had considered doing earlier on, might easily arouse suspicions: Mike Larman, arrived here just before the crime and departing so soon after it? Odd, perhaps? Incriminating even, maybe? And come to think of it he got in with Clare pretty quick, didn't he? Been out to Glaslyn, too, hasn't he, knows the lie of the land there. . . ? 'I want to help all I can,' he added, and laid his hand over hers on the wheel. He was a man who had successfully lived, and spoken, a lot of lies in his time. It was an accomplishment in which he had previously taken a secret pride. Now, travelling back to Greenways at Clare Shearer's side, a flickering sense of shame came to life inside him. But he misinterpreted it. Mistaking it for fear, angrily he snuffed it out of existence.

In the car-park at Greenways, Clare and Larman went their separate ways, he to pick up his hired Toyota and drive on to the library, she to go into the hotel. At the desk she enquired where her father was and was informed he had gone out, leaving a message for her that he would be with the police at Hereford and didn't expect to be back until about eight o'clock that evening. Also, the receptionist told her, Mister Curtis had arrived and had moved into the guest bedroom in the penthouse suite and hoped she would go up and see him as soon as she could. Banishing thoughts of going across to her bedsit to shower and change, she took a lift to the top floor.

'Jack! Oh, Jack, I'm so glad you're here!' As he opened the door to her she went into his arms in a rush and, for the first time since Natalie's disappearance, let down all the defences she had erected to hide the wild grief consuming her, to keep it inviolate from the public gaze. Burying her face in Jack Curtis's shoulder, she clung to him and wept.

Deeply moved, Curtis held her to him, stroking the tumbled, golden hair, speaking to her words of comfort although knowing that in truth there was no real comfort to be had. After a while, the storm of emotion wore itself out. Drawing away from him she dried her eyes and blew her nose, then went to the wall mirror and began tidying her hair.

'My father's with Inspector Dwyer,' she said. 'He doesn't expect to be back before eight. Will you be staying overnight?'

'Yes. London know this number; they'll contact me if necessary. I'll have to go back tomorrow, though. How is Hal? When he rang me just before he left to drive up here, he seemed as controlled as ever. Outwardly. Inside, he's suffering the tortures of the damned, we both know that. But I didn't press him. We understand each other.'

'He said he'll call me later this evening if there's any news.' Clare turned to lead the way into the sitting-room, saying over her shoulder, 'I think actually you're closer to him than I am.'

In regard to one particular part of his life I certainly am, Curtis thought as he followed her. And at that moment he swore to himself that never again would he give Hal Shearer any assistance whatsoever in the prosecution of his private crusade against the big guns of the narcotics underworld. For some while now he'd been questioning his own part in it. But that afternoon the whole situation came into sharp, cruel focus in his mind, because he had come to the conclusion that whatever had happened to Natalie, the people behind it were Hal's enemies, not hers. He believed now that somewhere along the line Hal had been discovered *and identified* by someone connected with the drug-trafficking fraternity as the killer who had visited death upon their kind on three occasions during the last ten years; and he believed that whoever that *someone* might be was now gunning for Hal, but had set out to inflict grievous mental and emotional torture on him before zeroing in for the actual kill. But Curtis kept all these thoughts to himself and intended to go on doing so for the time being.

'I could do with a coffee,' he said, as Clare sat down in one of the armchairs grouped on the far side of the sitting-room. 'Shall we make it in the kitchen here, or have it sent up?'

'Have it sent up, less bother.'

He rang Reception and placed the order, then asked her to bring him up to date on developments so far in the police investigation. 'All I know are the bare facts Hal gave me,' he said, 'and I didn't want to ask downstairs. Better to hear it from you.'

Concisely, breaking off only once when a waiter brought in a tray of coffee, served them and then withdrew, she told him the facts as known to her. 'So you see there isn't much to go on, is there?' she said miserably as she came to the end of it. 'God, I'm tired,' she murmured, and leaned back and closed her eyes.

Curtis went over to her and stood studying her. Usually so full of life, she seemed now bereft of it, her face pale and sad, her body listless. She looked, he thought, damaged, damaged deep down inside herself. And for a moment he was silent, only compassion and love in him. But he was careful to banish both from his voice before he spoke. 'I don't imagine Natalie had an easy night of it, either,' he said sharply, and was pleased to see her open her eyes and stare angrily at him. 'So come on, let's you and I talk this over, see if we can winkle out anything that might lead us somewhere. You can never tell what'll come out of thrashing a matter through, asking questions, going off after any hare you start up.' He smiled at her. 'I know what I'm talking about, Clare. It comes with the job. You'd be surprised at the number of times some seemingly peripheral little fact or happening opens up a fruitful line of enquiry. Shall we give it a go?'

'Great.' She straightened in her chair, alert again, eager. 'Better than sitting here glooming. It's worth a try, anyway. How shall we start?'

'By drinking our coffee.'

She laughed; and, satisfied, he turned away. Then for nearly half an hour, with Curtis prowling restlessly about the room, they tossed ideas, questions and answers back and forth between them with no useful result. Near to giving up, they decided to have a leisurely gin and tonic together and then, if they had still not unearthed anything promising, to give up, go their separate ways to get ready for the evening.

It was as Curtis handed her the drink that he started the hare which was to be, eventually, pursued to . . . a kill. 'You, know,' he said, 'whoever snatched her, it had to be someone who knew Natalie's habit of a walk on the hill every Sunday afternoon.'

'You can pencil in half the neighbourhood for that!' With a wry grin she sipped her gin, then looked across at him as he sat down facing her. 'I take your point, of course, but I don't see how it gets us anywhere. Talia simply doesn't *have* enemies, local or otherwise.'

'That can't be true, can it? Clearly she *did*.'

'Then I'd swear it's no one local. Which leaves us with the "otherwise".'

'D'you know of anyone from outside who's been to Glaslyn recently? Or around and asking questions, maybe? Questions about Natalie, about Glaslyn?'

'Well there's always people coming and going here – no! Wait a bit!' Suddenly Clare was on her feet. Looking up, Curtis saw her face tense with a fearful but puzzled misgiving. 'I can't imagine there's anything to it,' she went on, 'but *I* took someone new along to Glaslyn myself, just last week! This guy, he's staying here in the hotel, we'd been out together a few times and I asked Talia could I take him to her drinks do at the house.' She swung away from Curtis and began to pace about the room, frowning as she thought of Mike Larman, that very fun-to-be-with young man. Surely he couldn't be a suspect in this? Yet – she didn't really know him at all, did she? In fact, she didn't know anything about him except what he himself had told her! And he hadn't wasted any time in asking her out once he'd booked into Greenways, had he?

'Talia liked him,' she said after a moment, halting by the window, looking out. 'I like him myself. But you can never tell, can you? With someone you've only just met? And an outsider just visiting the area, he can give himself a false background easily enough, surely—?'

'For a while, he can.' Curtis went to her, laid a hand on her shoulder and swung her round to face him. 'So it could be worth us digging deeper here, Clare. This guy going out to Glaslyn, Natalie vanishing so soon after his arrival here – it's somewhat coincidental, isn't it? And coincidences tend to arouse suspicion in me; in my job I've seen too many of them turn out to be anything but. Tell me, what does this bloke do? What's he come to stay at Greenways *for*?'

'He's a freelance crime journalist, here to research local stuff for a series on rural violence.' Self doubt was plain on her face now. 'Well, that's what he said. That's his story. . . . Now wait! There's something else – maybe, just maybe! The day Talia was abducted, he was over in Leominster – or *so he told me*. Should we check on that, d'you think?'

'No. It'd take time, and quite likely we don't have a lot of that to spare. Better go first for the man himself. What's his name again?'

'Michael Larman. Does it mean anything to you? The kind of work he does, it might?'

'It doesn't at the moment. But, well, it seems to me it adds to the list of coincidences already standing against him. A crime reporter can acquire all kinds of information – all sorts of contacts, also. And it has been known for men of that ilk to use either or both for purposes other than writing up their stories. . . The trouble for us is that the coincidences could be . . . no more than the word implies. They aren't the sort of thing we can put to Dwyer and ask him to act on.' Curtis turned away and stood lost in thought, his head down. Then suddenly, his mind made up, he straightened his shoulders, finished his drink and put his glass down. 'Right!' he said. 'I'm off back to London!'

'London? What on earth for?'

'What we've got against Larman may not be enough to get the police going but it's damn well enough for me. OK, it's a long shot, a very long shot, I recognize that. But there's a chance it'll lead somewhere and I'm not going to pass up any chance at all, there's too much at stake. So, I'm for the Yard. I can be back there before ten o'clock, do some phoning tonight and set things up for tomorrow eight a.m. sharp.'

'You've lost me,' she snapped. 'Set *what* up?'

'Sorry, lass. Set up a session with the master computer. I'll feed it the name Michael Larman. In his line of work he might be listed, and if he is it'll flesh him out for me; it'll name others close to him, known associates, relatives and so on. There could be something useful to us in that. A lead to finding Natalie, Clare! It could give us a lead!'

Her face lit up with hope and she stepped forward quickly and hugged him; then stood back, her eyes shining. 'Go for it, Jack!' she said. *'Go for it!* And keep in touch, please. Waiting's hell.'

He tossed her his car keys. 'Bring the Clio round to the front while I get my things. And when your father rings, tell him what I'm doing, won't you? And, Clare,' – on her way out, she halted, turning to face him – 'should Larman make a move to leave, you make sure you know where he's going and how he can be contacted! Can do, without arousing his suspicions?'

She smiled a secretive, feline smile. 'Oh yes,' she said.

The evening Curtis returned to London, Alvar escorted Elena Fuentes out to dinner. On their return to his house in St John's Wood he took her coat and hung it up in the hall. She was in a good mood now, and he congratulated himself on that because she had been uptight and petulant at the start of the evening and he had worked hard to get her to relax. During their meal at the restaurant, he had kept the conversation away from business matters, talking about her dead husband Carlos, Alvar's nephew and while alive his most trusted collaborator. Alvar had loved the younger man deeply and after his death had drawn his family close to himself. Having fathered no children of his own he had come to regard the two boys as his sons, directing their academic and social education along lines which would enable them, in time, to take privileged positions in his organization. Elena had advanced no objections; her major consideration had always been to safeguard her own interests, and Alvar had satisfied those soon after Carlos's death by appointing her to his place in the consortium.

And very useful she had proved herself to be, he thought now, turning to her, smiling. 'Let us go straight into the study,' he said. 'Danielle will have put out the Rome documents there, ready for you to check the sensitive details before you sign. But I want the three of us to enjoy a glass of brandy together before the work. I told Danielle to wait up for us.'

For a second, Elena stiffened. Then she said, 'Very well,' and led the way through the house into the study, her faultlessly groomed head held high, her svelte body artfully set off by a calf-length silk dress the colour of which echoed the dark blue of her eyes.

Danielle had heard them enter the house. Wearing a copper coloured tunic of fine jersey over matching trousers, her dark hair loose, she greeted them as they entered the study, then went across to the drinks cabinet and poured three brandies while Elena and Alvar settled down in two of the three armchairs placed around the coffee-table. She had not wanted to join them. It seemed to her that recently Elena's ill-will towards her had intensified; also, that it had become more overt, especially in front of Alvar himself. Therefore, with only a week remaining before the execution of the series of Special Branch raids and arrests aimed at smashing Alvar's organization, she did not wish to spend more time with him and Elena together than she could help. With those closely co-ordinated raids so near, it was imperative she should not be exposed as an inside agent. However, Alvar had insisted she should wait for him and Elena to return that night. 'I wish the three of us to work together as comrades,' he had said to her that morning. 'I will not tolerate bad blood between you and Elena. You will *be* pleasant towards each other even if you do not *feel* so. We will start this evening. The three of us will enjoy a glass of brandy together in the study. And as we do so we will chat in a civilized fashion, no business, no personal remarks, simply pleasant and guileless chat. Then you will retire to your rooms, leaving Elena and I to complete our business.'

And that was what took place that night. But, as Danielle said goodnight to him to go up to her rooms on the second floor, and he saw her to the door, Alvar sighed. Then he took her hand and kissed it. 'Thank you for trying,' he said. 'Goodnight.'

Upstairs in her small sitting-room Danielle sat down and considered the disquiet troubling her. Never before had Alvar kissed her hand; and as he had done so she had thought that, for a split second, there had been an oddly calculating look in his eyes, and a suggestion of irony in the half-smile on his mouth. Did he suspect her? she agonized. Had her cover been penetrated? Was he playing her along while making ready to strike her down? A host of questions crowded inside her head and she was filled with a sense of foreboding. Her mouth tightened, her straight, dark brows drew together and beneath them the amber eyes clouded as fear and uncertainty invaded her mind. She shivered, and for a minute was consumed by a longing to call Caliban on the mobile phone locked away in her suitcase on the top shelf of her wardrobe. Caliban: the man who from the moment she'd gone under cover had been her number one contact outside in the real world. She had drawn from him so much strength – even simply from knowing he was there for her.

The moment of real fear passed, as had the others which had assailed her from time to time. The mobile phone was for use in emergencies only, for immediate life-threatening emergencies. And there were a mere six days to go now. Come next Monday, she thought, I'll be Justine Caine once more, the same as it says on my genuine birth certificate.

10

Situated ten miles out of Hereford on the Kington road, standing a little way back from a side lane branching off to the right of the highway, Rose Cottage stood alone, surrounded by pastureland. Originally it had been two homes, labourers' dwellings with a party wall between, but in the early eighties they had been bought by a property developer and converted into one residence. It was a good conversion though not inspired: large living-room, dining-room and excellently appointed kitchen downstairs, two *en suite* bedrooms and a fair-sized box room above. Its present owner had furnished it for letting, had a garage built on at the side, planted climbing roses either side of the front door and placed it in the hands of an agent in Hereford.

A week before Michael Larman booked into Greenways Hotel and made the acquaintance of Clare Shearer, a well-turned-out couple in their late thirties going by the names of Mr and Mrs Brown had viewed it, decided it suited their purposes, and hired it for two months.

'It's rather isolated,' the girl from the estate agency had said apologetically as she drove them out to inspect it.

'If we like it, that won't matter,' Mrs Brown had replied with a smile. She was a robust woman, attractive in an ordinary way. Her ash-blonde hair was luxuriant and elaborately coiffured (when she took her wig off at night her own hair showed dark and silky, cut in a short page-boy style). 'We're quiet people, and besides it's only a base for us while we house-hunt, find ourselves a property on the outskirts of the city.'

The Browns had settled in quickly, bringing with them little more than their personal clothing. They had begun house-hunting the very next day, and as they wanted a place south of the city the local residents saw little of them. For one thing it was a farming area and, in summer especially, its inhabitants had more pressing things to do than pay social calls on short-term tenants. Besides, it had soon become plain that the Browns preferred to keep themselves to themselves: they did not deal with the nearest garage, a mile away towards Hereford, alongside the main road; and they neither shopped at the little general store next to it nor gave their custom to either of the two nearby country pubs. As a result, the locals had paid little attention to them; therefore, when asked about them later, had practically no information to give. Which was just the way the Browns had intended it to be.

On the Sunday afternoon Natalie vanished from Glaslyn, the Browns drove three miles along the main road, towards Kington, and parked their grey Volvo estate in the layby designated by their paymaster, facing it back the way they had come. The layby was small and overhung by trees – a driver who did not know it existed would probably not notice it – but it was big enough for two cars. Mr Brown obeyed his instructions and was in position there by 5.30. Parking the Volvo in the middle of the layby to discourage unwanted fellow-parkers, he wound down his window and waited. The other vehicle arrived five minutes later. Mr Brown spotted it in his wing-mirror as it rounded the corner behind him and at once he moved the Volvo forward to give it room. The Land Rover pulled across the road, turned and backed up to him. He watched it in his mirror. The driver stayed put. The passenger got out and came round to him, a young, limber man clad in a far from new Barbour jacket, a dark base-ball cap on his head. He bent down and spoke through the open window.

'Greenways,' he said.

'Red route.' Mr Brown considered the password exchange childish, but – there had to be some way of establishing *bona fides*, and as he who pays the piper calls the tune, passwords were in.

'You open up the back of the Volvo and we'll carry her over – no, wait! Car coming, maybe!' But then they heard the approaching engine-noise switch direction and fade away, so they got on with the job. From then on the transfer from Land Rover to Volvo proceeded without interruption. As soon as it was completed, the man in the Barbour wished Mr Brown 'a safe stay at Rose Cottage', then he and his companion got back into the Land Rover and went off towards Hereford. The Browns watched them go, then drove sedately back to their hideaway. There they bore their tarpaulin-enwrapped 'guest' in through its yellow rose-embowered front door and upstairs to the carefully prepared spare bedroom.

From then on they cared for her well, washing and tending her at once, then putting her to bed. On the afternoon of the following day, they allowed her to dress in her own freshly laundered clothes and sit in the big armchair in the bedroom's bay window. Regularly sedated, she was no trouble to them at all. Nevertheless, they put their house-hunting on hold. 'My wife has a head cold,' Mr Brown told their estate agent, 'so I'm making her stay in bed.' He laughed then. 'Very hard work it is, too, to get her to stay there!' he added, and departed, smiling.

11

Having taken leave of Clare, Curtis was on the open road by 6 p.m. Usually he enjoyed the first part of the drive between Hereford and London, before he joined the motorway, taking pleasure in the lovely countryside through which it took him. But not so that Tuesday after Natalie vanished. As he drove his white Clio towards the capital to set about discovering whether the name Michael Larman existed within the comprehensively informed master computer to which his position allowed him access, Curtis was aware of none of the country glories spreading to either side of the roads he was travelling. His mind was possessed with fears. Fear for Natalie, who might or might not be dead, but who most certainly must be in mental torment and was quite probably in dire physical pain as well. Fear for Hal Shearer, suffering the tortures of the damned not only because of his mother's disappearance, and all the horrors concomitant with that, but also because of his secret and self-excoriating near certainty that his own outside-the-law activities were probably the root cause of it – surely *had to be*, Curtis agonized, for what other grudge could possibly have triggered such a vicious act? And lastly, fear for Clare, his deeply loved younger 'sister'. . . . As things were, Curtis thought, should his use of the master computer for a private investigation of his own result in him having to resign – if everything came out – so be it, he would accept his fate. Because *something* had to be done, and accessing the 'big feller' seemed to be the only course of action which might produce a lead, give them all something to work on.

A few miles beyond Burford, he pulled into a layby for a break. Getting out of the Clio he stretched, yawned, then unlocked the hatch and opened the lunch–box Reception had rustled up for him before he left Greenways. A flask of coffee, ham sandwiches, a Mars bar: moodily, he ate and drank, his mind still picking away at various aspects of the situation the Shearers had been pitched into, searching for leads which might have escaped notice. But he could discover none. The course he was following was indeed the only one open to him. It was a hell of a long shot, but worth a try.

He ate and drank until the box was empty, then tidied up and got in behind the wheel again. As he was about to switch on, his car-phone buzzed and he answered it. His caller was Clare. He knew at once, from her voice, that something bad had happened.

'What's up?' he demanded.

'There's been a development, Jack. Father came back to Greenways earlier than he'd said. He's had a message, well, not exactly a message, but—'

'Take it easy. No hurry. Just give me the facts.'

'Yes. Sorry. Father got this envelope. His name was on it – in block capitals cut out of headlines and pasted on one of those cheap manila envelopes – and it was just left on the desk here at the hotel, off at one end, behind a pile of guide books. No one saw it put there. One of the guests noticed it and passed it over to Jane.'

'What was in it?'

'A bit of one of her scarves, scissored off; and . . . and a lock of grey hair.'

'There wasn't a note?'

'No. Only the two things.'

'Is Hal sure the scarf's one of hers?'

'Absolutely. It's a big square, silk, with flowers on it. He bought it for her in Italy last year. The hair, I suppose it'll be tested but . . . he's sure, Jack. That's Talia's, too.'

'He's gone to Dwyer with it?'

'Yes. I told him you were on your way back to London, and why, and he asked me to let you know as soon as I could, so that's what I've done.' Her voice rose and harshened. 'Dear God I wish I could do something!' she cried. 'I've stuck at work, it's the only way to keep sane, but—'

He broke in, calming her with words of hope and love. He thought she was probably not finding much help in the former because to hope without there being some concrete reason for doing so is to live in a dream world whose ultimate collapse may destroy you. But he knew for sure that she was glad of the love and he gave it to her straight from the heart.

Then, assuring her that he would contact her or her father as soon as he'd got any results from his computer-search, if there were any to be got, he rang off and continued his journey. But Clare's call had brought Natalie's disappearance into sharper focus for him. The receipt of the scrap of scarf and the lock of hair – without an accompanying ransom note! – made it increasingly likely that she had been abducted and that Hal Shearer was the ultimate target of the exercise. More likely that the enemy, whoever it might be, was using Natalie to strike at *him*. If that were indeed the case, then surely there was only the one plausible reason for such a strike? Surely, it had to be because that enemy believed Hal to be responsible for the killing of one – or even, possibly, the entire score of three! – of the drug supremos shot dead in recent years with no one charged with their killings. Hal had been found out, and 'they' were intent on exacting revenge for those murders of their own kind. They had started with the abduction of Natalie – and who knew how that would end? – but they would not stop there. Of course not! Next would come Hal himself, or – nightmare thought – it might even be *Clare* next, and Hal the finale!

Now Curtis's mental agony twisted his guts, for if his reasoning was right then some of the guilt for what was happening to the Shearers lay with him. I should have stood out against Hal at the beginning, he upbraided himself, thumping his right fist hard against the steering-wheel – heard the squeal of brakes behind him, glanced up at the mirror, saw the bonnet of a truck right on his tail, huge and terrible *and gaining on him*— He wrenched the wheel hard over to the left and fought the Clio to a stop on the verge. He switched off and sat rigid, staring straight ahead as the truck careered on past him.

It came to a stop fifty yards on along the road. The driver dropped his head on the wheel, burying his face in his hands. 'Fucking bastard!' he muttered through clenched teeth. 'A fucking major-road-ahead sign staring him in the face and the sod drove straight past it, came straight out in front of me!' Then he scrambled out of his cab, pelted back along the road to the Clio and peered inside. As he did so Curtis wound down his window.

'*You!* – you all right?' the truckie asked, aggression draining out of him at the sight of the harrowed, guilt-stricken face.

'Yes. You?'

The truckie took a step back, rubbed a hand over his mouth. 'Yeah. What the fucking hell you think you were doing? You fall asleep or something? There's a halt sign facing you back there! You drove straight past it. Christ, I thought we were both goners!'

'Thanks be we're not.' Curtis made abject apologies then asked the truck driver whether he was going to lodge a complaint against him. The man gave a slow grin and said he was not, he'd goofed up in his time, too, and been forgiven for it.

'Reckon I'll probably goof up again,' he went on, 'so right now I'll store me up some brownie points.' He raised a hand in casual salute. 'So long, and . . . you watch out, mate!' he said, then jogged back along the road to his vehicle and climbed up into the cab.

Curtis restarted the Clio and drove on to London.

Leaving the library about six o'clock, Larman returned to his room at Greenways, showered and put on a clean shirt and trousers, then relaxed on the bed to read the newspaper, shoulders against piled pillows, legs stretched out in front of him. He had decided against calling Clare. He was deeply dissatisfied with himself, and found such self-knowledge, such feelings of guilt, hard to take. As he riffled through the sports pages in search of distraction, the telephone rang on the bedside table. Oh shit, that'll be Clare, he thought, what shall I say to her? Then he realized that more than anything else he wanted to see her; he swung his legs to the floor and picked up the receiver.

'Hello, Clare?' he said into the mouthpiece.

'Skinner here,' answered the gritty voice of his caller.

Skinner? *Skinner?* For a split second Larman rejected it; Skinner was not part of his present world, he wouldn't have the man in it. Then self-interest prevailed: best to keep Skinner on his side, he'd likely be a dangerous enemy.

'I've always got time to speak to a friend,' he said.

'Thought you would have. You ain't a fool,' Skinner said.

Larman caught a suggestion of threat behind the last remark and a vivid picture of the man's narrow face and knowing, pale-blue eyes came to mind. Watch your step now, he advised himself. 'Go ahead, then,' he said.

'Remember that little job we did together? Well, I got to wondering about it. See, I like to know who it is I'm really working for. I found out who financed it.'

In his hotel room, Larman grimaced, cursing under his breath. Then he thought, does it matter? Most likely not, so play it cool. 'So what?' he parried.

Skinner chuckled. 'I like you,' he said. 'You took my word for it straight off. Had you worried for a moment though, didn't I?'

'You did indeed. OK, you've had your fun. Now get down to the nitty-gritty.'

'Right. The lady we're talking about, her name's Elena Fuentes. And today an oppo of mine tipped me the word that the boys in blue are what you might call *interested* in her.'

'You'd told him about her?'

'Look, shut it! I believe in protecting myself, and I ain't asking your permission for what I do!'

'OK, OK. As long as you trust this bloke—'

'Shut it, I said! Now, you took on board the info. I just passed you?'

'I did. How serious is this interest in Madame Fuentes?'

'Very. It's supposed to be top secret but ... well, ways and means, as they say. My oppo's got contacts.'

'Is it on account of the abduction?'

'Can't tell. My friend ain't been sitting in on their briefings, y'know. He says it's more likely tied in with the drugs scene. But seems to me on the cards that the kidnap figures in it too, or might if the fuzz nab Fuentes. So I thought I'd fill you in.'

Larman shifted his shoulders uncertainly. 'Well, thanks, I'll—'

'Shit to the sweet talk. My neck's in this as well, remember?' Then Skinner chuckled. 'And there's another side to it,' he said slyly, 'you owe me now. Don't you forget that: any time I call the bill in, you better pay up, *mate.*'

12

On the Wednesday following the abduction, the Browns received the telephone call their paymasters had told them to expect early that morning. It came at 9.30. Mr Brown was in the sitting-room awaiting it. He picked up the receiver and identified himself under his present name.

'Is the woman in your care in good health?' asked a female voice, cold, peremptory.

So far in this job Brown had spoken only with men and for a moment he gave no answer, debating whether he should press his caller for further proof of her *bona fides*.

'Answer me!' the woman snapped.

'She's well.' Brown responded at once to the whiplash authority. 'We are keeping her sedated, as instructed.'

'No suspicions have been aroused, locally?'

'Absolutely none. I am certain of it.'

'If there is trouble, you know what to do and are prepared to do it?'

'Of course. That was in the agreement. I shoot her in the head and leave her lying, then we make our getaway from the cottage following the emergency procedure.'

'Good. Now listen. She will be removed from your charge this Friday. Expect my people at 10.45. A man and a woman, code name McKinnon. You will have our friend ready for them, sedated but able to walk with them to their car. That will be a black Toyota, and will be driven up to the front door of the cottage so you can carry out the transfer discreetly. As soon as she is gone, you two will vanish from the scene in the manner previously detailed to you. Is that clear?'

'Clear. Shall I—?' He broke off: the woman had terminated the call.

In a public telephone booth in Central London, Elena replaced the handset, cutting off Mr Brown's question. Going out on to the pavement she made her way along Regent Street, heading for Liberty's, walking as in a dream, her mind and soul absorbed in gloating over the corrosive fear and dread the man Shearer must, beyond a shadow of doubt, be suffering now. All the agents she had employed to ferret out his deepest emotional attachments had reported to her that he had but one: namely, a lifelong devotion to his mother. As she walked, Elena was wishing she could *see* Shearer at this time. She longed to reach inside him and touch/feel/*enjoy* the white-hot core of his torture as time passed and, in the absence of any news regarding his mother's whereabouts or state of health, he lay at the mercy of his own imaginings. Surely, she thought, those must be terrible? Surely, not having any idea of what is actually happening, he can't help but conjure up the worst possible scenarios? Is my mother hurt? he'll be wondering. Is she in pain, is she terrified, *is she dead*? Yes, he'll not be able to help himself, he'll have to confront and endure the emotional agony of each and every possibility his mind can conceive. As he does so, he'll be suffering as deeply and painfully as in the far past he caused me to suffer . . . and on Friday morning his dear mother will be killed. 'Mr and Mrs McKinnon' will collect her from Rose Cottage and she'll be dead by midday. The body will be stowed away in a hedge alongside a lay-by on whichever minor road the

McKinnons choose. If it's discovered, fine – he'll know then. If it isn't, we'll give it a few days then McKinnon will arrange for an anonymous phonecall to the police, point them in the right direction. . . .

Elena came out of her dream and found herself at Oxford Circus. Lifting her smoothly coiffured head she saw blue sky above her, then she lowered her eyes and contemplated the busy street-scene about her. She changed her mind: she did not go shopping at Liberty's as she had planned, she took a taxi home. Her mind and emotions were sailing on a lovely sea of vengeance in the process of being gratified. Sufficient unto the day are the pleasures thereof.

13

Hal Shearer was a tormented man. Fear for his mother's safety, guilt, and a blind ferocious anger were tearing him apart. When Clare told him that Curtis had gone back to London to run a computer check on the name Michael Larman, on the off chance of discovering some fact which might link him to Natalie's abduction, he had dismissed it as a one-in-a-million shot. But since then he had been obsessed with a desire for it to metamorphose into a reality. For if it did he would have something to work on, he could get down to hands-on action and force some truths out of the man.

But Wednesday passed without a call from Curtis, and during that night Shearer had little sleep. He had not telephoned Curtis, being sure that he would contact him when, and if, he had any news to give. But as he lay in bed he could not keep his mind off Larman, off the possibility that he might be involved in the disappearance. Yet – why should he be? Shearer wondered. And the only answer he could produce to that question was one which harrowed him: it has to be because Larman's deep into drug-dealing, and someone superior to him in that trade has marked me for my past three kills *and has used Larman to strike at me through Natalie!*

At first light he got up, showered and dressed, then went into the penthouse kitchen. Putting water to boil in the electric kettle, he spooned instant coffee and sugar into a mug. When the water boiled he filled up the mug and sat down with it in one of the two wooden chairs at the formica-topped table in the middle of the room. He had made himself a strong, sweet brew. Staring down into it he inhaled its fragrance – then in the sitting-room, the phone rang. He was by it at a run, lifting the handset, giving his name, all the time only one thought in his head, *Natalie! Let it be good news about Natalie!*

'Curtis here,' said the known voice.

'Jack. Good. What news?'

'Larman is a nephew of Elena Fuentes.'

'Je-sus! This could be the breakthrough! Are you absolutely sure?'

'Not a doubt of it. You see, Larman's on file because two years ago he was implicated in an insurance scam that went to trial. He himself wasn't charged but – well, there he is, complete with close family connections. The facts are indisputable: Fuentes was godmother to him, came over from South America. And Larman, he's a journalist all right, freelance for some while. Crime stuff, mostly.'

'So what I've been afraid of – it could be true, Jack! Somehow, Fuentes must've discovered I'm targeting Alvar, and she's hitting at me through Natalie.'

'You want me to check on Fuentes again? Last time, I dug back on her only from when Alvar took her into his organization, which was a bit after she married Carlos in SA. I didn't check her UK background, it never occurred to me it might be relevant.'

'No. Leave her till later. I'm going for Larman and – Christ! I'm going for him hard! The filthy bastard, worming his way into Glaslyn though Clare—'

'Cool it, Hal. That Fuentes is his aunt is no proof he had any part in the abduction.'

'It gives me the right to work on him and find out if he *did* have a hand in it! And if he did I'll have out of him every single thing he knows about what's happened to Natalie. I believe she's still alive, Jack. I have to. So – I'll get the truth from him. He'll spill; I know ways. And when he does, God granting she's still alive I'll go get her.'

'Well, there's one good thing will come out of this, you'll have to drop the Alvar killing.'

'Like hell I will! You're right off beam, my friend. What's happening gives that added rightness. Also, it enables me to see my way clear to my next job: it'll be Elena Fuentes.'

'But if your move against Larman pays off, and you free Natalie, perforce you'll expose Fuentes to Dwyer and his people. Then the Langley Manor meeting'll go by the board, your Alvar hit with it—'

'You're in error. I shan't bring the authorities into it.'

'They *are* in it. You'll have to work through Dwyer with anything you get out of Larman.'

'No. I'll work alone,' Shearer said, the very quietness of his voice seeming somehow to convey the suppressed violence consuming him, even to emphasize it. 'The police have to work by the book, as I know only too well. Me, I burnt their book of rules long ago, page by bloody page.'

'But – dammit, watch your step, Hal.'

'If you were here with me, Jack, would you help me do the sort of thing we both know will almost certainly have to be done to Larman to get the truth out of him?'

There was a pause before Curtis answered. Then he said, 'Yes, I would. But I have to say, too, that I'm damn glad I'm *not* there. Remember, we don't know for sure he's involved in this.'

'What, with him coming up here and getting in with Clare so fast? He's involved all right. And I'm going to work on the assumption that he knows what happened to Natalie and, probably, where she is. Count on it, Jack: I'll get what I want from Michael Larman.'

'Is he still at Greenways?'

'Yes, Clare said he's staying on a bit. Right, I'll get started on this. Oh, one more thing: don't tell Clare about Fuentes, will you? OK? Good. I'll be in touch later. And – thanks.'

Going back into the kitchen Shearer stood by the table and, wrapped in thought, drank his coffee. By the time he had finished it he had the details of his plan of action clear in his mind. Naturally, parts of it would have to be played off the cuff, according to Larman's reactions as the scenario Shearer envisaged for him progressed.

But Shearer had no doubt he would get what he wanted. Rinsing his empty mug at the sink he thought with grim satisfaction, I think 'persuasion' such as I have in mind would probably break *my* resistance in like circumstances, and I doubt Larman's any tougher than me. Then he went back into the sitting-room and rang through to Clare's room in the annexe. His call woke her up and when she answered she protested sleepily that it was only 6.30 and most decent folk were still abed.

'But there's some around who aren't decent,' he said dourly, 'and it seems likely your Mike Larman is one of them – no, no questions! I've had an anonymous phonecall and I've a lot to tell you, also I need your help. Get dressed quick as you can and come up here.'

'Do I have time to shower?'

'Is Larman a crack-of-dawn man? In the mornings, does he take off early?'

'Just normal, from what I've seen. He usually has breakfast a bit after eight—'

'Then forget the shower.'

'You're on to something?' Hope and excitement were building in her voice. 'It's about Talia?'

'I hope. Hurry, now. *Hurry*, girl.'

14

In his room at Greenways, Mike Larman replaced his phone, hooked his thumbs into the belt of his chinos and, head down, paced moodily to and fro alongside the bed. Clare's call had worried him; he had hoped to be out of the hotel on the day's work without meeting her, but now she had asked him to go up to the penthouse suite straightaway. It wouldn't be for long, she'd assured him, she was on duty at nine o'clock, but she wanted someone to talk to. They could have coffee and a chat – he always cheered her up, she'd said, and right now she needed that badly. Listening to her, Larman had felt as if she was there in the room with him, attractive vital girl, hazel eyes that at times had looked at him as if he were the only man in her life. He had said he would go up at once – but as soon as he'd put the phone down he wished he hadn't, wished he'd excused himself, he could've pleaded he hadn't got the time, could've—

The hell with it! He halted in his tracks. You've just told the girl you'll go, so cut the bullshit and go! But see you keep your distance from her – not only while you're up in the penthouse with her but also from now on. You can't have her in your life, get that into your cretinous head. You're in too deep with Elena for that.

At 7.40 he knocked on the door of the penthouse apartment.

116

Clare opened it to him, bright hair drawn back from her face and tied with a narrow black ribbon, a white silk blouse tucked into the waistband of her side-slit, beige skirt. Smiling to him, she greeted him warmly and led him into the sitting-room.

'Come on over here and sit down,' she went on, walking straight across to the fireplace opposite the door, where, on a table beside one of the armchairs, he saw two mugs and a pot of coffee on a tray.

He followed her, sniffing appreciatively. 'Coffee smells good—'

'Hold it there, Larman, I've got a gun on you!' Peremptory, the male voice came from behind him and he stopped dead in his tracks, mind and body frozen in a moment of total panic. 'Good. And by the way my gun's got a silencer so don't gamble on my being afraid to use it up here. Now, stay as you are till I say otherwise,' went on the cold, hard voice, and Larman knew the man was coming up behind him, the footsteps were soft on the carpet but every nerve in his body was strung screaming-tight, his skin crawled with fear – then he turned his head a fraction of an inch and saw that the man holding the gun on him was Hal Shearer, *Natalie Shearer's son.* In that moment of recognition he realized with sickening certainty what it was Shearer wanted from him, and two hard truths about himself stood clear in his mind, one negative, the other – perhaps? – peculiarly positive, given his situation. The first was that he'd been a fool and a rat to put himself in hock to Elena Fuentes the way he had. The second was that having done so, he would not easily betray her. After all, Shearer couldn't know much—

Shearer had stopped in front of him, facing him, the Mauser trained on his heart. 'Where is she?' he asked, quite quietly.

'I don't understand this.' Larman met the flinty-grey eyes steadily, for, after all, what he had just said was true, he had no idea why Elena sought to afflict Shearer the way she was doing.

Keeping his eyes fixed on Larman's, Shearer spoke to his daughter. 'You go now, Clare,' he said.

Looking across at him she saw his face as the face of a stranger, a man of violence, a man she could not relate to; and a fearful loneliness engulfed her.

Her father sensed the anguish in her. For a moment it puzzled him, but then he realized why it was there. 'I'd kill for Natalie, if that were required of me,' he said.

She nodded. 'Yes. I hope it won't be.'

'It won't. I've seen the method of persuasion I have in mind for him used once, and that was on a man in a league of toughness light years in advance of this guy's. It works, and it works fast.' His voice hardened. 'Go now,' he said.

Clare left the room without another word. 'Now you and I can get down to business,' Shearer went on, as the door closed behind her. 'Natalie Shearer, abducted last Sunday from out near Glaslyn. Is she alive?'

'What makes you think I know anything about it?'

'The fact that Elena Fuentes is your aunt.'

It jolted Larman severely. His mind in turmoil, he dropped his eyes, hoping for time to think.

It was denied him. 'I've got you up here for one purpose only,' Shearer continued without a pause, 'namely to find out if my mother's alive, and, if she is, where she is now. I'm convinced you can answer both those questions and I'm not going to waste time explaining the background to the situation. There's a witness, Larman. It's not common knowledge yet, but I've been spending a lot of time with the police and I was with them when this woman rang in. She's a local, and she's an ornithological freak. She was out on the hill last Sunday afternoon, had her binoculars with her. She's a rich lady, they're really something, those glasses of hers, very powerful indeed. If I name you to Dwyer – well, it's highly likely she'll be able to identify you, place you on scene that day. So here's my offer: you give me what I want and I won't do any naming. So I'm asking you, *is Natalie Shearer alive?'*

Shearer was lying about the witness. But Larman had no way of checking that; besides, he knew himself guilty and fear had him by the throat: Shearer's face, set in a mask of barely controlled fury, gave him no hope. 'Yes, she's alive,' he said. 'She's being held prisoner.'

Shearer searched his eyes and decided he was telling the truth. 'So what was done to her, out there on the hill?' he asked.

'She was knocked out with a stun gun.'

'You bastard! And – the blood?'

'Her forearm was cut with a knife.'

'Why?'

'I don't know. It was orders.'

With a massive effort, Shearer restrained his rage, his urge to hit out, to see Larman's blood flow as his mother's had done. 'Does Fuentes plan she stays alive?' he asked.

'I don't know.'

'Is that the truth, or just to get yourself off the hook?'

'It's the truth, I swear!'

'She's being held prisoner, you said. Where?'

'No.' Larman shook his head and looked away, seeking to hold on to the rags of his pride. 'You'll have to go to Elena for that. The whole ploy was hers, I never knew the reason for it, or what was to happen after we grabbed her.'

'Go to Elena? You fool, I've no time for that! I intend to free my mother today and you're going to help me by telling me where she is and every damn thing you know about the circumstances in which she's being held.'

'No, I can't *do* that!' The cold sweat of fear was on him. 'Elena would kill me—'

Shearer gave a harsh bark of what might have passed for

laughter but for the cruel set of his face. '*Elena*? You're shit-scared of her, aren't you? Well, you're probably right to be, but you'll have to deal with her later. She's not here with you: I am, so it's me you've got to be afraid of. You're going to tell me where my mother is.'

'*No!*' Paralysed with fright, he was hanging on to the simplicity of plain denial. '*No!*' he said again—

And Shearer reversed the Mauser and went for him, smashing a swingeing blow to Larman's jaw, following on with a savage strike to the back of the head with his weapon as the man went down.

Larman crashed to the floor and lay still.

When Larman came to, raising his chin up off his chest, opening his eyes slowly, painfully, he perceived he was in the kitchen of the penthouse suite at Greenways. The curtains were drawn across its one window, and the ceiling light filled the room with brilliance. Cautiously, he took stock of his situation. He was seated in a straight-backed wooden chair and there was a gag in his mouth. The chair was wedged securely into the corner nearest the door, and he was trussed to it with nylon cords. One of these went three times around his waist and the back of the chair; a couple of others lashed his ankles to its two front legs; a fourth tied his wrists together behind the slats of its back. And he was naked from the waist down.

Opposite him across the kitchen, he saw Shearer standing with his back to him at the yellow work-surface running the length of the wall there, atop a row of storage cupboards. He could not make out what Shearer was doing. Then abruptly the dull ache inside his head sharpened, stabbing at him with such ferocity that he closed his eyes against it, praying for it to stop. After a minute it lessened and he opened his eyes again. As he did so, Shearer turned and saw that he was conscious. 'Good,' he said. 'Now we can get to work.'

But Larman was staring in dawning horror at the electric kettle standing on the work-surface, a little to Shearer's right. In reality the kettle was of medium size, but to Larman at that moment it was the only thing in the room he was aware of and it was huge. It was metallic green with a gold trim, a thin wisp of steam was coming out of its spout, *and he had realized what it was there for.*

'Yes, I've just boiled it up,' Shearer observed conversationally. Larman's reaction promised well, he thought. 'I'll tell you what's going to happen,' he went on, going across to stand in front of him. 'I ask you a question, then you nod your head for yes or shake it for no.' He smiled thinly. 'Who knows, we may even get to where we are certainly going to get to, without a drop of boiling water being *spilt*. Whether it is or isn't doesn't matter to me, but it will to you, I think. Anyway, we'll see. I'll give the kettle a boil-up so it's ready if we need it, then we'll start.'

He switched the kettle on again, then came back; stared down into the bruised face of the man he had tied to the chair. Larman stared back at him because he found it impossible to look away. Then the kettle switched itself off, and Shearer asked his key question for the first time. He was sure that once he had forced Larman to give him a 'yes' to that, he would have broken his will to resist; the man would have surrendered as such and would yield, would give him sufficient information for Natalie's rescue to be effected.

'We're both aware that it's in my power to cause you agony,' he said, 'and take my word for it I'll gladly do so to get out of you the facts I want. But I won't hurt you if you co-operate. So the choice is yours. It's time for you to make that choice. So I ask you, if I take the gag out, will you tell me where she's being held?'

Fear and despair harrowed the pale-blue eyes, but Larman shook his head. At once Shearer swung away, strode across to the kettle. Lifting it off its stand he brought it to the chair to which his prisoner was bound. Larman's shirt front hung down between his legs, but his thighs were bare. Shearer laid his hand lightly on the one nearest to him and then withdrew it.

'That's where it'll hit you this first time,' he said. 'Change your mind?'

The blue eyes shifted to the wisp of steam drifting out of the spout of the kettle. Then he looked up and shook his head again. His face was white.

Shearer lowered the kettle until its spout was two or three inches above the exposed thigh, then tilted it. A gout of scalding water streamed down on to the tanned flesh. Violent spasms of pain convulsed Larman's rope-clamped body. Eyes screwed tight shut he flung back his head, jerking it from side to side, his neck muscles corded taut as the screaming inside him fought to get out only to slam up against the gag and be forced back down into his lungs. His chair juddered against the floor and against the walls to each side of him as his torment scourged him but they kept it upright, he was imprisoned there, he could not escape.

Gradually he fought pain to a standstill. Shearer watched him for a second, then topped up the kettle at the sink, replaced it on its stand. When that was done he went back to stand in front of his prisoner, regarding him impersonally. He thought of him exclusively as the man who had assisted in Natalie's abduction and therefore could tell him where she now was, and thus ensure her rescue. On that count he saw Larman as fair game; by committing that crime he'd given up all rights to fair treatment. Looking down at him now, he neither felt pity for him, nor was he troubled by any feelings of guilt at the methods he was using to get what he wanted out of the man. The only feeling in him was impatience for Larman to regain sufficient control of himself to answer coherently and to the point.

Quite soon he judged him able to do so: the spasms that had been racking his body had subsided to tremblings, and although he sat limp and exhausted, chin on chest, his breathing had returned to normal. Reaching out his right hand Shearer gripped Larman's jaw hard and forced his head up. The man's eyes were closed. 'Look at me!' he ordered. Slowly, the eyelids lifted. Shearer saw the light-blue pupils were misted over with tears of pain. He was pleased then, thinking, I've *got* him, I'm nearly there now.

'Are you an imaginative man, Larman?' he enquired. But the pain-remembering eyes stared vacantly up into his own, and the swollen lips did not move. 'Come on, you can answer that!' he said roughly. 'Nod for yes, shake for no, that's all I'm asking you, so *come on!* Answer me!' He dug his thumb and fingertips cruelly into the flesh of Larman's jaw, leaned closer. 'Are you an imaginative man? Yes or no?'

Larman nodded.

Shearer straightened up. '*Thank* you!' he mocked. 'So, you are an imaginative man. In that case I suggest you use your imagination now. Because I'm about to boil the water again and the next time it's going over your balls. Think about *that*, Larman. *Imagine* what it'll feel like, what it'll do to you and yours.' Then he let go of the bruised jaw, strode across to the kettle and switched it on once more. Keeping his back to his prisoner, he stood waiting for the water to reboil.

Larman watched him as though mesmerized. He was telling his brain to get to work, to find some way out of his desperate situation, but it was not responding. Blind terror absorbed the whole of his sentient being: he imagined the kettle being tipped; he imagined the steaming water cascading down out of it towards his own flesh – but then came only a sort of roaring chaos inside his head. He could not imagine the reality of what would happen to him then; and he found that even more will-destroying than imagining it.

The kettle came to the boil and switched itself off. Shearer picked it up and went back to his captive. 'D'you know, I've learned something about myself this morning,' he said to him, peering down into the blue trapped-animal eyes that couldn't look away from his. 'I've never done this sort of thing before, and I was worried I might find it a bit hard – you know, unpleasant, shaming even. But I don't. It's easy.' He smiled. 'Still, I don't suppose you're interested in my moral decline at the moment,' he went on. 'Let's proceed. The water's just boiled, I'm ready to pour it out, I've only got to push your shirt aside and – well, you can say goodbye to a lot of things because you're going to get a big dose this time. But I'll give you one more chance before I do that.' He tilted the kettle slightly and a small jet of water dropped down on to the inflamed, already blistering skin of Larman's thigh. 'Will you tell me where she's being held?' he asked.

Larman's head jerked back in shock, his eyes clenched shut, his entire body tried to thresh about but it could not. The pain was driven back into his mind and he felt as if his brain would burst. Surfacing out of agony with only one desire in his mind he forced himself to stillness, looked up at Shearer and – nodded.

15

Shearer had many good friends in the Hereford area, quite a few of them making their living from the rich arable land surrounding the city, breeding livestock, cultivating the fertile soil they had been born to. It was not his habit to make use of his friends, but he did so that morning without a moment's hesitation. As soon as he had milked Larman of all he knew regarding Natalie's present whereabouts and the circumstances in which she was being held, he sat down in the penthouse sitting-room and thought out his plan of action to free her. It seemed to him to have a good chance of success, but it was plain to him he would need some local help; so he went across to the phone and set about getting it. His first two calls were abortive, they were answered by employees who informed him that none of the family was at home. The third time, he was lucky.

'Margaret Bonington here,' said the familiar Herefordshire-accented voice, and Shearer was glad to the roots of his being because Mags was just what he needed now. With Mags, a friend only had to ask and provided what was requested was within the bounds of her capabilities, it would be done or given at once and without question. 'Any news of Natalie?' she asked.

'Nothing more than I told you yesterday. Listen, Mags. This is to do with her, though, and I have a favour to ask you.'

'Name it. If can do, will do.'

'I want the loan of either your Sierra or the Range Rover for the whole of today, and I want it now, as soon as possible.'

'We won't be using the Range Rover. I'll bring it over to you myself. Ten o'clock now. Be with you in half an hour, OK?'

'Wait! One other thing, no, two actually. Are those marigolds still rioting away in your lovely garden?'

'They are.'

'Then could you please pick me a big bunch of them, with maybe some of that thin stuff that grows in spikes, yellow flowers, mullein, isn't it – oh hell, Mags, anything, I want a bunch that looks as if it's just been picked from the garden.'

'Count it done. And what's the second thing? A sack of potatoes?'

He laughed, which did him a lot of good. 'You're closer than you think. Could you bring a lettuce, some courgettes, broad beans? Stick them and the flowers in one of those trugs you have and bring it over when you come.'

'Right, I'm with you, Hal. You want a country-neighbour gift.'

'Exactly.' Country neighbour? he thought bitterly. Yes, that's what those bastards at Rose Cottage are posing as, for sure, and hopefully that will help bring about their downfall. On that thought adrenalin surged through him. 'Hurry, Mags,' he said. 'For God's sake, get here as soon as you can. And don't let anyone know about this, will you? Staff, family – *no one.*'

An hour and a quarter later, Shearer was behind the wheel of the Boningtons' green Range Rover, well out of Hereford, on the Kington road. On the passenger seat beside him rested the plaited-reed trug Mags had brought with her. It looked very bright and attractive: tucked in at one end of it, the sunshine colours of a large bunch of marigolds and mullein gave brilliant contrast to the various greens of the fresh vegetables arranged in with it, a cos lettuce, courgettes, broccoli and broad beans. On top of the courgettes lay a white envelope addressed to Mr and Mrs Brown, which contained a card inviting them to drinks with a (fictitious) Ann and Bob Morgan at Broadridge Farm the following Saturday evening.

Larman had not known the exact location of Rose Cottage. The only information he had been able to provide was that it lay about ten miles out of Hereford, on a side road branching off the A480 to Kington, that it was a two-storey building and that it did indeed have roses around its front door. So, coming to a garage about nine miles out of the city, Shearer pulled in to its forecourt, went into its shop and bought a box of Black Magic chocolates. The girl behind the counter was young and attractive, with glossy brown hair, hazel eyes and a wide, unpainted mouth. As he handed her a five pound note, Shearer said he was looking for Rose Cottage, Mr Brown who lived there had told him the side road to it was about ten miles out of Hereford, but he had not come to it yet. Had he far to go, he asked, or had he missed the turn-off?

The girl smiled at him. 'Some people just don't take care to give you proper directions, do they?' she said, as she put his change into his hand. 'Weird, people are sometimes, aren't they?'

'In your job here, you probably meet quite a few oddballs. I hope you don't get too many real thugs, as well.'

'Some.' She smiled at him again. 'That kind, they just make the nice ones more welcome.'

'And the Rose Cottage turn, I haven't passed it?'

'Oh, sure. No. It's about a mile further on, on your left. You'll see a stand of sycamores right by the road; it's just beyond that, you can't miss it.' She shot him a quick grin, adding, 'Famous last words, they say, but truly, you really *can't* miss it if you've got eyes in your head. Turn off there and the cottage is a few hundred yards on, it stands back from the road, there's a short drive to it.'

Shearer thanked her and went back to the Range Rover, thinking, well, she's the last civilized human being I shall see this
afternoon until I set eyes on Natalie. Now for Mr and Mrs
Brown.

A few minutes later he saw the sycamores, and a little way
beyond them he turned on to the side road leading off to the left,
verdant arable land spreading wide around it, a couple of farm-
houses visible a mile or two away. Then he saw the cottage
ahead of him. It was set back from the road with a gravelled
drive leading up to its front door just as the girl had said.
Turning on to that he drove slowly towards the house, taking
rapid but searching stock of its frontage as he went: one room
either side of the doorway, and a two-car garage built on to the
side, a black Volvo parked outside it; on the upper storey, two
big windows and a little one between them, presumably to light
a stairway. Climbing roses planted either side of the front door
swarmed over walls and trellises, the entire front of the house
was awash with yellow blooms.

It was 1.45 p.m., and Mrs Brown was in the dining-room of Rose
Cottage. Dressed in tailored cream trousers and a nut-brown
blouse, she was clearing condiments from the table and putting
them away in the sideboard. Hearing a car turn into the drive,
she crossed to the window and looked out. The visitor was
driving a Range Rover, she observed; it was newish, clean and
shiny. Some bloody neighbour or other, I suppose, she thought,
so I'd better play it cool, dream up some excuse or other to get
rid of them politely. The car pulled up well short of the front
door. Watching, Mrs Brown saw a tall, dark-haired man get out
of the driver's seat. Hatless, rangy-looking in chinos, black
sweatshirt and a hip-length denim jacket, he stood still for a
moment, his head up as he studied the front of the cottage. He's
admiring the roses, thought Mrs Brown, deciding he looked

rather interesting after all. Then he turned away, went round to the passenger's door, opened it, reached in and lifted something out. As he walked towards the house she saw he was carrying a trug loaded with vegetables and a country-sized bunch of flowers. Dear God, I'll have to ask him in, she thought, he'll have seen the fucking Volvo, I'll have to or it'll look odd and we don't want people talking. Then the front doorbell rang and she went to answer it, pausing at the hall mirror to smooth her hair into place because . . . well, the visitor was a good-looking guy and her life had been decidedly dull that way lately.

Shearer could be a smooth operator socially, when he so chose. It was a skill he had deliberately set out to perfect, on deciding to carve out a career for himself in the hotel business. Now he practised it successfully on Mrs Brown, introducing himself as Robert Morgan of Broadridge Farm across on the other side of the main road and informing her that he and his wife ran stables and a riding school there. They were having a few friends in for drinks in two days' time, he said, and his wife had sent him over to welcome the Browns to the neighbourhood in proper country fashion – he gave the trug into her hands – and invite them over, the formal invitation was on top of the courgettes. Mrs Brown smiled and suggested he come in for a coffee, if he had the time. When he said he had, she was pleased.

Shearer stepped over the threshhold of Rose Cottage. He found himself in a small hall. Doors stood open to left and right of it, and straight in front of him a flight of stairs led, obviously, to the upper floor. Mrs Brown ushered him through the door to his right.

'I hope your husband's at home,' he remarked, as he entered what was clearly the sitting-room. 'It'd be nice to meet him too.'

She put the trug down on a side table. 'He's just started work in the back garden. I'll go and call him in through the kitchen window,' she said, then turned to her guest with a smile, 'Do please—'

'Hold it there!' the man said, and she broke off, stood rigid with shock. "Robert Morgan" was standing facing her. He had a gun in his hand; it was trained on her heart and it was silenced. These facts slammed into her mind, then she looked up at his face. It was set in hard, bitter lines and his grey eyes bored into hers, merciless and resolute.

'I've come to take the woman you're holding prisoner here,' he went on. 'Do as I say, and neither you nor your man will get hurt. Resist, and I'll put a bullet into you. I'll do whatever has to be done, I'm not leaving without her. If that means we end up with blood on the floor here, it'll be yours. Clear?'

White-faced, her mouth slightly open, her arms hanging loosely at her sides, Mrs Brown nodded, then the self-excusing words came tumbling out. 'The deal was there'd be no violence. Don and me, we don't do violence, never have, we do con jobs—'

'Are there any guns in the house?'

She nodded again. 'One. It's a .32, it's in the desk over there on your left, the top drawer. It's not loaded. We don't—'

'Shut up.' Keeping her covered with his Mauser he removed the .32 from the desk drawer and put it in the pocket of his jacket. Mrs Brown's eyes were riveted on him. Her overriding priority was to get herself and her husband out of this horrible situation with their skins intact therefore she decided to do exactly as the man with the gun said, at once and without argument.

'Now, come over here and stand in front of me,' Shearer ordered. 'Good. Hold both hands out at arm's length in front of you. Right. Place them together, with your palms and your wrists touching.'

Mrs Brown obeyed his commands to the letter. When she had done so he pulled out a two-yard length of nylon cord from his pocket. One end of it was already fashioned into a running noose, and he slipped this over Mrs Brown's hands to encircle her wrists, then drew it tight. Holding the free end of the cord, he pushed his face close to hers and stared into her eyes. She sensed the suppressed will to violence in him, and shivered.

'Where's your prisoner?' he demanded.

'Upstairs,' she answered dully. 'First bedroom on the left.'

'Is she tied up? Hurt in any way?'

'Oh no, no! Like I said, Don and me, we don't do any violence. The lady's sedated, just. We've looked after her well, she's perfectly all right—'

'It'd better be true.' Shearer stepped back a little. 'Now, you and I will go into the kitchen. Will the window be open?'

'Yes.'

'Then you go to it and I'll stand off to the side – with the gun, remember. I'll still have you on the cord, and it'll be tight. You call your man inside. What's his name?'

'Don.'

'So you say, "Don, we've got a visitor, a neighbour. Come in and meet him, we'll be in the front room". Got that? You can say it word for word?'

'Yes.'

'See you do, because if you don't you get a bullet. One last thing: is he likely to argue? Not want to come in?'

'Oh no. He's digging and he hates it.'

The ghost of a smile hovered on Shearer's lips and was gone. 'Let's go, then. The moment you've said your piece, you come away from the window.'

In the kitchen, he looked out through the window and saw a stocky man with a shock of dark hair working outside, about twenty yards off. His back was to them, he was wearing a light-blue T-shirt over jeans, and he was digging over a strip of bare soil between the cottage and the lawn beyond. Shearer stepped to one side and motioned Mrs Brown forward. She went to the window, called out her given words to her husband.

Hearing her summons, Don Brown stopped digging and turned round, his perspiring face breaking into a delighted grin. 'Sweetest talk I've heard today,' he answered. 'I'll be with you in a couple of minutes.'

Crunch point imminent, thought Shearer, and dug the barrel of his gun into Mrs Brown's side as she returned to him. 'Get back into the sitting-room quick,' he whispered. 'Go, woman! Go!'

She went, and he followed close. Leaving the sitting-room door slightly open behind him Shearer spoke to her quietly. 'Go over to the far side of the room,' he ordered, 'and stand by the bookcase there, side-on to the door so Don'll think you're having a conversation with your visitor who's across from you and out of his sight. I'll have the gun trained on you and if you make sound or movement to warn him, I'll shoot you. For me, it's just as easy that way; for you, it wouldn't be. Understood?'

Stiff with fear, she nodded. 'I won't do anything. I promise I won't,' she whispered. 'Don't hurt me—'

'Shut it. Just do as I said. Remember, one false move and you get shot where it hurts.'

Mrs Brown obeyed his instructions. Shearer transferred his gun to his left hand, he shot sufficiently well with that, if necessary. Then taking Brown's .32 out of his pocket he gripped it by the barrel and positioned himself behind the part-open door, listening to the sounds Don Brown was making as he came in to meet his visitor. He heard the back door close, then a brief pause punctuated by muffled movements. Brown changing into house shoes? Shearer wondered. Then came the sound of water running as, undoubtedly, the guy washed his hands. That noise ceased, there was another pause. Tidying of hair? Then Shearer heard footfalls approaching along the carpeted hall, towards the sitting-room – and shifted his balance on to the balls of his feet, raising Brown's gun in his right hand up to shoulder height.

Brown came in through the half-open door, smiling, eager, and saw his wife standing side-on to him across the room. 'Jean,' he said, advancing towards her, 'so sorry to have kept our guest—'

Shearer stepped forward and hit him from behind, bringing the handgrip of the gun hard down across his skull. Words died sudden death in the smiling mouth, Brown pitched forward and lay sprawled senseless on the floor. Across the room, his wife spun round and cried out, made to go to him.

'Stop right there!' commanded Shearer, and she froze, whimpering, her face contorted with rage and grief. 'Like I said earlier, you do as I say and neither of you gets badly hurt; resist me, and you will. Are you going to play ball?' She nodded. 'Then lie down on the floor just where you are, on your back,' he went on. 'If you kneel down first you'll find you can do it with your hands tied.'

Mrs Brown's prime directive in life had always been to act entirely in her self-interest at all times. She followed it now, and four minutes later was stretched out on the floor on her back, gagged with one of the two men's handkerchiefs and tape her captor had brought with him for the purpose, the cord around her wrists fastened in a slightly different way and her legs taped together at the ankles. Soon after that her husband lay similarly bound and gagged, Shearer using another length of cord from his pocket to secure him at the knees as well. As he finished doing so, the man opened his eyes. They rolled in his head as his mind sought explanations for his predicament, then fixed fearfully, questioningly, imploringly on Shearer who had got to his feet and now stood looking down at him.

Shearer shook his head and turned away. Going across to the woman he stood staring into her eyes. 'What you said about my mother, you'd better be right,' he said grimly. 'If I find you *have* hurt her, the two of you will pay for it before I leave.' Then he turned on his heel, strode out into the hall and raced up the stairs two at a time, thinking, God be with me in this, God grant she's safe.

First door on the left, the Brown woman had said. Reaching the landing he turned left, opened the door facing him and saw – Natalie. She was sitting in a wing chair the other side of the room, between the disordered bed and the window. She was dressed in her beige needlecord trousers and overblouse, her hands clasped loosely in her lap, her head drooping chin on chest and her eyes closed. For a split second he stood stock still, staring at her, drinking her presence into himself through his eyes. It really is Natalie, he was thinking, she's here in front of me *and she's mine*: all that's left to do now is to take her home.

As that slow-motion light-flash of time blazed in glory in him, this certain knowledge made the world for Hal Shearer a marvellously good and lovely place to be in. Then he went to her, crossing the room to kneel at her side.

16

In the penthouse at Greenways, Clare and her father were in the sitting-room. It was 5.35. Parking Mags Bonington's Range Rover in the car-park of the hotel about an hour and a half earlier, with the trug of flowers and vegetables returned to its place on the front seat, Shearer had helped his mother into the foyer and then, with the assistance of Clare and another member of staff, had taken her up to the private suite. There, Clare had taken over. Shearer had showered and changed. Now, in grey trousers and white shirt, tie loosely knotted, he listened as Clare reported that Natalie seemed to be recovering fast, that she had insisted no doctor be called, and had had to be persuaded to go to bed and rest.

'Actually, two minutes after her head touched the pillow she was sound asleep,' she ended, smiling across at him. 'So how about a drink? A bit early, I know, but – heck, I could use a whisky, and I bet you could too!'

Shearer poured the drinks. 'We've got time now, Father,' Clare said, looking soberly up at him as he handed her her glass, 'I asked you some questions this morning, after you'd told me Mike Larman was involved in Talia's abduction and you wanted me to get him to come up here. I asked you, how you knew, and you said you'd just had an anonymous phonecall. You said the caller said he was speaking from London, told you that if you wanted to find your mother Michael Larman could tell you where she was; also, that if you went to get her then a) you mustn't go in your own car because it was under surveillance by the abductors, and b) if you informed the police she'd no longer be there by the time you arrived. But then when I asked you how Mike fitted into the thing, you said there wasn't time to explain it all to me. That was true *then*. But it isn't true now, is it, so please – how and why did Mike get involved in this?'

For a full minute Shearer stared at her in silence. She could read nothing in his eyes, his face. Then he said, quietly, 'No. Sorry. Some day, maybe. Not today.'

After a minute of rebellious anger, Clare accepted it. He's been suffering, she thought. I have to give him space – which, science will have us believe, is another dimension of time. 'Then at least tell me what happened this afternoon,' she said. 'Blow by blow, how you got her back.'

But he drank some whisky and turned away, a ferocious anger against Elena Fuentes, against Robert Alvar and all their kind, boiling up inside him. He controlled it, just. He knew it of old, it was that same violent gut-rage that had over the years powered his vendetta against the big men of the drug-trafficking underworld.

'You're thinking of the Browns?' Clare had seen his face before he turned away and his expression appalled her. 'You wish you'd—'

'Not them. Not even Larman. They were nothing, cat's-paws only.'

'Who then? To make you look . . . like that?' To make you look capable of murder, she thought. No, it's worse than that: you were *lusting* to kill. That's what I saw in your face—

'Leave it!' he said.

She did so. She loved him, and perceived him warring against private demons. You keep out of this, it's mine alone – that's what he's saying to me, she told herself. Well, he has the right. She looked down, wishing she could get close to him, knowing she never had and resenting that knowledge.

Shearer sat down in the armchair opposite hers, put his whisky on the table beside it and dropped his head in his hands. Slowly, the fury inside him slunk back into its lair deep in his psyche. But it had named its prey: Elena Fuentes, who, it seemed, had somehow linked him with his past kills and was now zeroing in on him intent on revenge – had already made a strike against him, via his mother. You will be the next for me, Fuentes, you bitch, he thought. There's only three days to go to the Alvar kill now. I won't waste any time after that, I'll have you before you can strike at me again. . . . But as he thought this, a strange thing happened. Inside his head a still, small voice proclaimed, quite suddenly and with great clarity: after Alvar, you should put aside the gun for ever. . . .

'Please, Father, tell me about Talia.' Clare spoke across his thought-word *gun* and he looked up, across at her. For a moment then she caught in his eyes an expression she had never seen in them before, a strained, haunted look as if he were saying inside himself *I've had enough*. And she thought, I don't have the faintest idea what was in his mind just then before I spoke but I ought to have, I'm his daughter – and now, for the first time ever, I believe he needs me to understand . . . something that's of great importance to him. What is it he's 'had enough of'? If only I could say the right thing now, I think he'd tell me.

But before her brain could discover 'the right thing', the customary cool watchfulness was guarding his eyes once more. He smiled at her. 'Yes, I'll tell you about Natalie,' he said, then raised his glass. 'First, though, here's to Mags Bonington; if she hadn't come up with the necessary so fast probably a whole day would've been wasted.' He was never to know that, had that come to pass, his mother would have been gone from Rose

Cottage by the time he got there, and dead within an hour of her going.

They smiled at each other, and drank. 'Now, where do you want me to begin?' he asked.

'Where the Brown woman let you into the cottage.'

Shearer told his story well. He was always observant of detail in respect of people and places, and he had a retentive memory. And to his surprise he found himself quickly caught up in the drama of it, reliving his tension and anxiety.

'So I got up off my knees, lifted Natalie out of the armchair, carried her downstairs and out to the car, then helped her in,' he said as he came to the end of the story. 'She was amazing. She was smiling by then, even talking a little. The sedative must have been wearing off; she was probably due another dose. . . . D'you know, I don't think I've ever felt so happy in my life as I did on that drive back here together. Not that we said much.'

An intense delight spread through Clare. And me, I don't think I've ever felt so happy as I do at this moment, she thought, to have you let me see you so moved, and hear you speak from the heart. But she was not sure enough of herself to tell him so. 'And you drove off from the cottage straightaway, then?' she asked carefully.

He shook his head. 'No. I couldn't, much as I wanted to, there were still things to be done in there. I went back in and told the woman that the way I'd tied her hands together left her able to use them, if she kept at it. "Untie your own feet", I said, "then do your husband. It'll take time, of course. I'll be way beyond your ken long before you're both free. What you do after that is your own affair. You can phone your employer and spill your story, or you can beat it while the going's good".'

'You were taking a bit of a risk, weren't you? They might be there for days, might die—'

'I was just coming to that. I told her that whatever she decided to do, they'd better get a move on as I'd be phoning the Hereford police at six o'clock.'

Clare smiled. 'You're wonderful,' she said, *'everything's wonderful.'* She picked up her drink and finished it. As she put the glass down she asked, 'That call from London, didn't it cross your mind it might be a hoax?'

'I'd be a fool if it hadn't. But given the circumstances I'd have followed up a hundred hoax calls on the chance of one of them being on the level.' He stood up and went across to the phone. 'I'll ring Dwyer now,' he said.

Clare frowned. 'And for Mike that'll be the end of the ride.'

'No. He's gone back to London. Signed out at midday, Reception said.'

'But—'

'After I'd got all I wanted from him I told him to clear out before I got back. I don't want him in this, Clare. In fact, I want the whole affair kept as quiet as possible, it's very bad for business – bad for us personally, too, it'd drag on for months. So I shall simply tell Inspector Dwyer that my anonymous caller from London this morning gave me all the information you and I both know I actually got from Larman.'

For a split second she sat frozen, then suddenly she burst out laughing, a wild sense of freedom and relief flooding through her. She laughed until the tears came, then brushed them away, leaned back and smiled at her father's back as he rang Dwyer.

Tidying the boxes of chocolates on the shelves behind her counter, the girl with brown hair and hazel eyes heard the siren of the police car sound briefly as it approached from the Hereford direction. She went to the windows overlooking the garage forecourt to watch it pass by. It was only doing about fifty, she judged, so no high drama, worse luck. A woman police officer was driving it, she observed, and for a moment she daydreamed about how she herself would look in one of those smashing hats, and what the guys were like when you got to work with them. Then she looked at her watch and smiled dreamily. It was 6.25, so there were only five minutes to go and then ex-Corporal Jock McKay the evening-man would come on duty and she'd be free. She'd drive off into the sunset; it was disco-night at the Waggoner's Arms.

WPC Merrick was twenty-six years old. Five feet eight in height, she had an athletic figure and a broad-browed, regular-featured face. A faint, semicircular scar on her lower left cheek showed where, at the age of ten, she had been kicked by a pony. Easing the police car to a stop a few yards short of the front door of Rose Cottage, she switched off, slid out from behind the wheel and stood studying the house, settling her hat firmly on her short black hair. In the car, Sergeant Mason called in to report that they had arrived on scene and were about to investigate, then he got out and joined her.

'Looks dead quiet,' he said. 'Doors and windows all closed, garage ditto.'

'Could be a set-up?'

'More likely a hoax. Come on. Front door first.' The sergeant stepped up to it and pressed the bell, hearing it ring inside the house.

They waited, listening for sounds of movement within. None came. 'Looks dead quiet': the words said themselves over again in Merrick's head and *dead* lingered on after the others had faded away. She frowned, then put her head close to the door, her ear almost touching it as she strained to hear the sounds she wanted to hear, sounds of life. But she heard . . . nothing.

'Somehow I don't think this one's a hoax,' she said.

He grinned. 'You getting bad vibes again?' he joked, then reached out and pressed the bell a second time. And again, they waited. Rose Cottage waited with them. Set sweetly amidst wide acres of fertile and richly cultivated land, embowered in yellow roses, it rested silent beneath the early evening sunshine.

'You can hear the bees in those fucking roses,' Mason said, suddenly annoyed by the sound.

'Why don't we try the fucking door?' Merrill retorted. She loathed swearing, but believed in giving it straight back if you got given it.

The sergeant did so and it opened. Going inside they went through the house room by room. Throughout, it was clean, tidy and empty of personal belongings. No clothes in the wardrobes, no soap or toothpaste in the bathroom, no tissues or hairpins on the dressing-table.

And no person anywhere; living, wounded, or dead.

17

Twelve o'clock the following day, Friday, found Alvar, Elena Fuentes and Danielle Fraser gathered in the study of Alvar's house in St John's Wood. Sitting round his rosewood desk they were discussing the report he had received the previous morning from Gutierrez, detailing the progress he had made in their Bristol 'constituency'. Things were going well there, apparently. This greatly pleased Alvar, and Danielle echoed his praises of the younger man. Elena diplomatically but somewhat absentmindedly did likewise, her mind and emotions deeply engaged elsewhere. For by now, according to the arrangements she had made, Shearer's mother would be dead, her body lying abandoned in a hedge alongside some suitable layby not too far from Rose Cottage. It would probably be discovered soon. . . . Perhaps it has been by now, Elena thought, and sat back in her chair, a faint smile on her face as she felt out and revelled in the suffering that would assail Shearer when he learned of his beloved Natalie's death. Perhaps he knows already and is even now experiencing what it's like to have someone you love deeply snatched from you, dead, finished for ever so that you know you'll never again—

The telephone shrilled. Danielle went across to the table beside the window and answered it. She listened for a moment then turned to Elena, saying, 'Yes, she's here with me now. Hold the line, she's coming over.'

Elena took the receiver from her. 'Madame Fuentes speaking. Who is that?' She rested one impeccably manicured hand on the table, painted red nails tapping it – but then, abruptly, still. 'McKinnon?' she exclaimed in utter disbelief. Then again, 'McKinnon?' she repeated, and turned her back on Alvar and Danielle.

But they had seen her face go pinched and white. They glanced at each other and then looked down, Danielle at the file open in front of her on the desk, Alvar at his hands. Both listened avidly as Elena's call continued. However, they did not learn a great deal from the one side of the conversation they could hear, for it consisted mainly of her asking questions, and she was taking care that the phrasing of them did not reveal to those with her in the room too much detail of the matter she was discussing. Nevertheless, her body-language as she took in information, and the varying tone of her voice as she herself spoke betrayed to them the enormity of the shock she had received.

'So where are you speaking from now?' Her voice was controlled, but fear seethed beneath the surface. . . .

'Thank God you had the good sense to leave the place at once and call me from elsewhere.' Relief in her now, the fear quietening. 'What state was the place in when you arrived?'

'Car in the garage?'

'You are certain there was no note? Nothing?' The incredulity was still in her voice, but it was clear that she was beginning to realize that the impossible had actually come to pass.

'And there was no sign of any *difficulty* anyone might have had?' But then as she listened to some explanation from her caller, her nervous impatience flared out of control. 'No, wait!' she interrupted. 'I must talk to you in private. Give me the number you're ringing from. I'll call you back in five minutes on my car phone.' She noted down the number, replaced the receiver, tore the slip off the notepad. Turned to Alvar then, her face still pale, the dark-blue eyes jewel-hard.

'A personal matter,' she said, stiff with the effort of preserving an outward show of calm. 'Nothing important really, but you know how such things are. I must deal with it at once, find out what's going on.'

'Of course, my dear.' Alvar was on his feet. 'Our business for this morning is routine, we can attend to it when Danielle and I return from Sutton. We aren't leaving until five o'clock this afternoon, of course, but I have other things to attend to between then and now. I will not be in the house.' And uttering solicitous platitudes he escorted her out to her car.

When he came back into the study, Danielle looked up at him from the document she had been reading. He seemed puzzled and uncertain, she thought, which surprised her since she had seldom before seen him either. Sitting down opposite her across the desk, he leaned his forearms on its polished surface and frowned at her.

'I am coming to believe that Elena is engaged in some private matter which is of enormous importance to her,' he said thoughtfully. 'I do not like that. Twice in the past she has made use of me to help her when some private agenda of her own has run into trouble. I have no intention of doing so again, should it come to that. She imagines that because she is family to me I ought to assist her in whatever she does. But I do not see things in the same way. She is not *of my blood*, so it is different. Should she get into difficulties in some extra-mural activity, I will not have her drag me into it this time.' He leaned back, passing one hand over his white hair. 'If she chooses the bed, she must lie on it,' he added with a faintly suggestive smile.

Self-pleased bastard, aren't you, thought Danielle, giving him a small and enigmatic smile in return. But her curiosity was aroused by what Alvar had said. He knew Fuentes far better than she did. Suppose the woman was indeed running some secret agenda of her own, it would be prudent to glean some idea of what it might be. 'When you're working undercover don't let any opportunity to acquire inside information pass untaken, even if at the time such info. appears to be irrelevant to your own remit.' So Caliban had said to her once, and she'd found it paid off. Besides, she recalled, earlier on she'd had her own suspicions regarding possible private plottings by Fuentes – and who knew, they might actually be relevant, they might be directed against one Danielle Fraser!

'You mean you suspect she might be working against you in some way?' she asked Alvar, pretending she had not understood him. 'Surely she'd never—'

'Not against *me*, no, she would not dare!' He shook his head, too engrossed in his own thoughts to notice that Danielle was apparently, and most unusually, being obtuse. 'This time I find myself intrigued, because what appears to be causing her such angst does not seem to be connected with her position within the consortium. On the two earlier occasions it was, but she was not working against me, she was simply attempting to manoeuvre herself closer to me, the boss.'

'Then what's she engaged in now?' Danielle prompted his silence. 'Have you any clues?'

'Only Elena herself. She is . . . she has gone away from me. In her mind, her heart. Gone away from me, from her life with Carlos, from the boys Carlos fathered on her. All her energies, her emotions, seem to be given to something else, something far back in her past, I believe.' He glanced across at her, a sharp, probing look. 'Do you understand what I mean?' he demanded.

She sat quiet for a moment, her head down. Then she looked

up at him. 'Yes, I think so,' she said. 'But what I don't understand is why it should worry you so much?'

Alvar did not like that. His full mouth tightened, his eyelids drooped over his dark eyes. He stared at her coldly. 'And you, Danielle, why should *you* be so interested in what Elena may or may not be doing?' he asked, an edge to his voice.

Take care, woman! she warned herself, this man's deeply guileful, and not easily deceived. But I'm not going to let this go easily, it could matter. So, smoothing back her dark hair, she smiled sunnily and answered him with what was, in parts, actually the truth. A truth. As far as it went. 'Because I have your interests at heart, and it seems to me she may be threatening them,' she said, then carried the fight to him. 'And also because I am grateful to you, Robert Alvar,' she went on. 'Thanks to you I have a stimulating, well-paid job and I am working for a man who has admitted me to his confidence. More than that, a man I have come to think of as my friend.'

She removed the smile from her face. '*Are* you my friend?' she challenged him. 'Are you truly my friend?'

At once he relaxed. 'Have no doubt of it, Danielle,' he said. 'Forgive me. This present difficulty with Elena, I feel a need to get to the root of it; it is poisoning the relationship between she and I.'

'It's to do with something in the past, you said. Before she married Carlos, d'you mean?'

'I suspect so. But nothing I discovered in that part of her life would account for her present state of mind.'

'You've had her investigated, then? Vetted?'

'Naturally. I had that done many years ago, first when Carlos informed me he desired her as his wife, and again before the marriage contract was drawn up. Originally I was displeased with his choice. I tried to persuade him to wed closer to home and more usefully.' He smiled. 'I was wrong in that,' he went on.

'In fact, Elena has proved an invaluable asset to the business. But recently she seems to have become . . . not entirely wholehearted in her commitment to me, to the consortium. As I said, it is as if her true self is given elsewhere, to some secret and personal affair.'

'But surely she'll tell you what's troubling her? She's a member of your family, the mother of your nephews who are like sons to you.' But even as she spoke she saw Alvar's eyes veil themselves against her. Watch your step, Danielle! she cautioned herself again. Don't take risks in this. *Alvar's* continuing confidence in you is your top priority. So drop Elena's affairs rather than arouse his suspicions by your interest in them.

But Alvar chose to continue with the subject. 'You are right,' he said blandly. 'She has indeed confided to me the outlines of this personal affair she is engaged in. But recently it seems to be getting in the way of business, it is bringing unwelcome outside attention to us, and that I will not allow. If she goes too far I shall call her to heel.'

'What is it, this personal affair of hers?'

'Why do you wish to know?'

Danielle laughed and got to her feet. 'Oh, it doesn't really matter,' she said. 'Womanly curiosity, I suppose. I don't like Elena, as you're well aware, but I'd like to know what makes her tick.'

His eyes glinted with amusement as they met hers. 'It would give you the upper hand over her, you think. You knowing her secret and she unaware that you did. You would enjoy that, I believe?'

She nodded. 'Nice people, women,' she said.

'The gentler sex, of course.' Then suddenly he sat up straight in his chair and went on, speaking now with a harsh, clinical detachment. 'Elena had one brother,' he said. 'He was a drug-runner. When she was twenty he was shot dead in the course of a narcotics raid in London. His killer was a police officer. It was an act she has never forgotten and never forgiven. Now, twenty years later, she is planning revenge for her brother's death. "Blood for blood". I, Roberto Alvarez, I understand that, and I sympathize with it.'

Danielle stared at him, stunned. But she recovered quickly and looked down to pick up a file, saying, 'Yes, I can imagine Elena doing that.' Then, raising her eyes to his again. 'What's she got in mind?' she asked, with, she hoped, the requisitely casual degree of interest. 'Does she plan to kill this man herself, or will she put out a contract on him?'

'The latter, I believe.'

'Who is it she's gunning for, I wonder? D'you know?'

'Yes, I know.' Alvar stood up and came round the desk to her, took the file from her hands. 'I know, but the name is classified information,' he said, smiling into her face. 'The general picture, that I am happy to share with you, Danielle, but the details of a matter so closely bound up with my family's honour? No. That is for Elena and I alone. So now you and I will have an early lunch and then I will go out.'

Soon after Alvar had left the house, Danielle walked to the local High Street and entered one of the telephone kiosks outside the post office there. Lifting the handset she tapped out her contact number.

'Oberon,' she said into the mouthpiece.

'Calling who?' asked the known voice.

'Caliban,' she said. 'What luck, getting you straightaway.'

'What gives? La Señora not giving you trouble, I hope?'

'Don't be so damned laid back! Trouble for someone it may well be, so listen and take heed! Maybe if you'd bugged her place when I asked you—'

'It wasn't possible,' he interrupted curtly. 'After your earlier call I had a further check run on her but nothing came up. I'd have let you know if it had. So OK. Now, give.'

She could see him in her mind's eye, cool, calm and collected. He was, without doubt, her friend. He was also her personal link with the 'outside' world, he carried weight in that world and when it was required of him he got things done there fast, efficiently and, when and if necessary, ruthlessly. Through him, if what she had gleaned from Alvar was indeed true, she might possibly save a man's life. If. Might. Nevertheless—

'I think I know why Fuentes has been so worked up lately,' she said. 'She's planning a killing.'

'Who's the target?'

'That's what I hope you'll find out.'

'To what purpose?'

'To prevent her succeeding.'

'OK. Give me what you know.'

In the kiosk, Danielle smiled: good for Caliban, as usual he trusted her judgement as to whether tangential information should or should not be acted upon. 'It goes back to 1978. That year her brother was shot dead by a police officer in the course of a narcotics raid. She's gunning for the officer who killed him.'

'In person, or a contract job?'

'I don't know for sure. Alvar clammed up on me then. I didn't press him.'

'Wise girl. Bigger things at stake.'

'But you'll work on it? This police officer, whoever he may be – it seems his life is under threat.'

'Any idea of the timing involved? Long term, or short?'

'Impossible to say, as of now. I'll try to find out more—'

'No! You hear that, *no!* You stick to your own job. Don't do anything to jeopardise Alvar's trust in you. Alert Control via emergency channels if there's any change in his planned visit to Langley Manor.'

'But you'll work on this killing Fuentes has in mind?'

He caught a peculiar urgency in her voice and asked, 'Why should you care so much?'

'I just do. Maybe I feel for him. She's a bitch and she's out for his blood. She'd be out for mine if she thought she'd get anywhere, she's so jealous of my standing with Alvar. She wants me out of her way and she believes in going for what she wants, no holds barred—'

'Cool it. Three days from now she'll be behind bars and you – you'll be Justine Caine. Where shall we go to celebrate, you and I, on Monday night? After it's all over, when Alvar, Fuentes *et al* are safely locked away? That's unless you've got a string of other guys lined up—'

'I have not, as you well know. How could I, anyway? How about La Maison d'Or?'

'Your wish is my command. And as for La Señora's proposed victim, I'll get to work on it at once.'

'I'll ring you back?'

'Yes. Give me half an hour. After all there can't have been many fatal shootings by police officers in London in '78.'

Danielle went into the nearest café and ordered a coffee. While drinking it she wondered exactly why she'd done what she had. Then she let her mind idle over what kind of man the policeman in Elena Fuentes's sights was: speculated on what he looked like, how he'd been affected by his killing, what he was doing in his life now. The half-hour passed too slowly for her, and she rang Caliban five minutes earlier than arranged.

'His name's Shearer,' Caliban told her.

'Any more about him?'

'He left Special Branch that same year, went into the hotel business and now has interests in both the UK and Spain.'

'Well, he'll be safe from her for a while, won't he? Provided he stays alive till Monday.'

'Safe *for a while*, yes. But obviously La Señora harbours a grudge for ever. I doubt she'll give up on settling this one.'

18

Saturday, and Glaslyn lay basking in the sunshine of the summer morning. Some distance from the house, Hal Shearer and his daughter were at work clearing ivy from the path through the woodland bordering the river. To their right, thirty yards away across greensward, the water ran smooth, sparkling in the sunlight. On their left, the land rose gently and on this bank periwinkle and ivy flourished in open spaces between the trees.

Clare dropped her secateurs and straightened up, easing her back, casting a longing glance at the water. Her jeans were green stained at the knees, the sleeves of her yellow cotton shirt were rolled to the elbows and her face was beaded with sweat. 'Isn't it time for a swim yet?' she called to her father.

A few yards ahead of her along the path, Shearer sliced off an invading streamer of ivy with his billhook, balled it up and chucked it into the waste basket beside him, then peered at his watch. 'Body says a vehement yes, but timepiece says no,' he answered, turning to her, rubbing the back of a grimy hand across his mouth. 'We promised Natalie we'd finish the path, let's do it. No reason we shouldn't take a break, though. Sit down and cool off, have our coffee.'

'Wacko, I love you!' Clare sped off towards the river, to the spot where they had left a groundsheet, their swimming gear, and a large thermos flask. Watching her, Shearer saw her stop there and stand looking out over the water, her corn-gold hair shining in sunlight. She's beautiful, he thought. Not to everyone, of course. Who is, to *everyone*? To me, she is. But then, I love her. That colours it, I suppose.

Suddenly she turned to him. 'Come *on!*' she called impatiently. And at once he looked away from her lest she intuit his love for her.

They sat down side by side on the plaid groundsheet and she poured their coffee and they drank thirstily, gratefully. Then Clare put down her plastic cup and stretched out on her side, propped her head on one hand and looked across at her father who, forearms resting on bent knees, was gazing across the river.

'Great, isn't it, the way Talia's simply picked up life from where it left off for her last Sunday, six days ago,' she said.

'They're doing the honey today, I think. The one culinary speciality in which our expert Mrs Richards has to bow the knee to her.'

'I wish you didn't have to go back to London today. And couldn't you at least stay till after lunch?'

'No. Business.' Then he turned to her. 'Does it hurt, Clare?' he asked. 'Larman? The way he used you to get to Natalie? Did he ... did he matter to you?'

She had no difficulty in holding his eyes. 'No,' she answered. 'I liked him, no more than that; but I'm glad he's gone. Glad, too, that you kept him out of it, told the police that it was the guy who rang you from London who gave you all the stuff about Rose Cottage.'

Slowly, he smiled at her. 'You should be more careful about your men in future, maybe.'

It made Clare feel good that her father should reveal even that much of his feelings to her. But she was determined it should go deeper, on her side at least. I want him *to know me*, she thought, I want us to talk ideas, perceptions.

'What Larman did was shitty rotten, yes,' she said, 'but people make mistakes, don't they? I think it's possible he regrets what he did – not because he lost out in the end, but because looking back on it, he thinks he was rubbish to do it. And also, it could be that pressure was exerted on him, couldn't it? Forced him to it? It might've come about that way?' She looked away from him. 'I'd imagine extreme pressure – monetary, maybe, or emotional, moral, whatever – well, it could, it *might* make a criminal of almost anyone. D'you think?'

Shearer was glad her eyes were no longer on him. Because as she spoke her last sentence, setting before him her way of thought on the issue of criminality, there came in him a strong desire to tell her about his personal vendetta against drugs barons which had led him to commit acts which were without a shadow of doubt heinously criminal. Yet even as the longing was born in him, his ingrained habit of reticence sprang to life and attacked it. That she was no longer looking at him weakened his longing and strengthened its attacker: the yearning for confession died a swift death and Shearer closed his eyes and sighed with relief. He stretched his long legs out in front of him, put his hands palm-down on the ground either side of his hips and rested his weight on them.

'Larman certainly reacted to the pressure *I* exerted on him,' he observed. 'He broke, totally. And thank God he did.'

'But Father,' Clare said, frowning, 'this isn't going *to go away*, is it? OK, you won, you got Talia back unharmed, but is it over now? Or will it happen again?' She was talking her forebodings alive, her imagination was filling future days with terrors and they showed in her eyes.

Seeing her haunted by fear harrowed Shearer. 'I'll deal with it!' he snapped. 'Leave it, Clare! Nothing like it will happen again, I'll make sure of that! I'll—' But he broke off as a man's voice hailed them from the direction of the house.

'Hey! Where are you?' Curtis's shout came to them through the woods. Swiftly recovering his composure, Shearer scrambled to his feet and started up towards the path, saying they'd better not be caught skiving.

Appalled by his outburst, Clare crammed down the sense of disorientation it had aroused in her, sat up, put a smile on her face and stayed where she was. 'Well I'm going to skive a bit longer, and to hell with Jack,' she called after him. 'Tell him he can use my secateurs and help you.'

But Curtis, who had claimed three days' overdue leave and was spending it at Glaslyn, brought a message for Shearer: Natalie requested her son's presence at once in the workshops, something to do with the July honey order for Greenways.

'I'll go up straightaway,' Shearer said, quite happy to do so. 'You'll stay and help Clare finish the path?'

'Sure, no sweat—'

'You think?' And with a grin Shearer turned and set off through the woods, heading for the kitchens.

Jack Curtis sat down beside Clare, refusing her offer of coffee. 'What's up?' he asked.

She looked away. 'What makes you think anything's "up"?'

He gave a wry smile. 'Useful, rivers can be. For staring at when you don't want to talk face to face.' But all he got was a stubborn lift of the chin; she would not look at him. 'It's to do with Natalie, isn't it?' he went on after a minute or two. 'She's safe back home now, though. It's over, Clare.'

'But – is it?' She turned to him suddenly and the angst he sensed in her cut him to the heart. '*Is it* over? Or is it – whatever *it* is – all out there still? Because we don't know *why* the thing happened, do we? So what if whoever's behind it strikes at us again? That's what's ripping me up, Jack. They might hit us again any time, and for God's sake how do we live with that?'

'Natalie seems to be taking it in her stride.'

'She's got her bleeper, she's got the emergency phone number, and everyone in the valley's rallying round; they're all on full alert to keep tabs on her welfare. Sure, I'm aware of all that, and I know she feels OK with things the way they are. But me, *I don't!*'

Curtis's mind, his heart, his very life had been bound up with those of the Shearers for many years. By now, not only did he know them all profoundly, also, he had come to a keen understanding of their attitudes and feelings towards each other. And, he loved them all. Out of these perceptions and awarenesses he said to Clare, 'This is about Hal really, isn't it? About *him* and the abduction. Tell me what's just been going on between you.'

'Yes, it's about that. Like I said, I'm afraid there may be more of the same to come. Just before you called to us I was going on at him about it – and suddenly he clammed up completely! "Nothing like it will happen again, I'll make sure of that!" he said. And there was something about him as he said it that frightened me. He was so *angry*, Jack! Deep-in-the-blood angry . . . *killing* angry.' She shivered, and looked down at the grass. 'I think my father knows more than he's told us, or the police, about *why* Talia was snatched,' she went on, her voice low, the words coming out jerkily. 'In fact, I'm sure of it. "I'll deal with this myself", he said. And as he said it his face, his eyes – I've never seen him look like that before. He was . . . he was all violence. It scared me, his face then. I was looking at my father and seeing a man I didn't know.'

'And didn't want to know?' His voice was as quiet as hers.

There was silence for a little while. When finally she spoke she did not answer his question. 'I think he's holding something back from Talia and me, Jack,' she said. 'Somewhere in all that's been going on there's something he knows but hasn't told either of us. And I think p'raps you know what that something is.' She looked up, straight into his eyes. '*Do you?*' she asked.

Then for the first time in his life, Curtis lied to Hal Shearer's daughter. It did not come easily out of him, the lie. He had to force it out; and, as he did so, he realized and admitted to himself that he was doing so because he could not bear the thought of being the one who apprised her of her father's guilt. . . . Well, love doth make cowards of us all, he mocked himself sadly, and said to her, holding her eyes and imparting to his voice a casualness that was not in his heart, 'No, I can't think of anything he might have kept back from you. Things'll work out, Clare. Just give it time.'

Not saying anything, she searched his face; then she gave him a cool smile and stood up. 'Come on, there's work to be done,' she said brightly, and pointed up to the path. 'See there? It's nearly finished, that last bit won't take us more than ten minutes. Then me, I'm for the river. You too?'

'I never miss the chance, you know that.' Scrambling to his feet he followed her up the slope. But he was a tormented man, and as he slashed away at ivy with the billhook, then crammed the cut, leafy trailers into the rubbish basket, he agonized over what had just been said between Clare and himself. He'd lied to her concerning a matter of supreme importance. He'd had to, hadn't he? He couldn't simply say to her, Oh by the way, your father has killed three men in the course of the last ten years, sorry I didn't get round to letting you know about it earlier on. . . . Surely *he'd had to* lie?

Too late, too late by now to do anything other than lie, he told himself as they swam in the cool, lazy-flowing river. I ought to have told her years ago— No! *No, by God!* I'm on the wrong track altogether – I should have *withdrawn my support from Hal* years ago! Well, yes. Hindsight's such a bloody awful gift, isn't it? Sure it is. And where does it leave me now?

Curtis found no answer to that question; and he had neither the time nor the opportunity to do anything about it that day since

Shearer left Glaslyn before lunch, ostensibly for a meeting, but in fact to drive on south of London, to Sutton. But by the time he departed that afternoon – he was scheduled to fly to Amsterdam on official business that evening – Curtis had come to one diamond-hard decision: he would continue to do everything in his power to persuade Hal Shearer to call an end to his murderous vendetta against drug bosses *while he was still in the clear.*

But: 'But, will he still be in the clear after tomorrow?' whispered the jeering little voice which seemed to have taken up residence inside his head . 'The hit on Robert Alvar – what if it goes wrong? Hal's had luck and the element of surprise on his side for all his previous kills, but what if they fail him this time?'

The Talisman, a café-bar near the entrance to Ealing Underground station, custom-furnished for the casual trade: at 11.30 that Saturday morning, while Shearer was cutting back ivy in the woods at Glaslyn, Caliban walked in off the street and bought himself a cup of coffee at the counter. He had spotted Croft as he came in; the Special Branch man was sitting at a table at the far end of the room. He joined him, putting his coffee on the table between them and folding his long, lean body neatly down into the chair facing him.

'What the hell is that?' he asked, pointing at the steaming mug in front of Croft.

'Bovril.'

Caliban gave a slow grin. 'You hardly need body-building stuff.'

'An unoriginal remark.' At sixty-one, Croft was heavy-bodied without being flabby. As one of Caliban's contact men within Special Branch, he had worked with him on the Alvar undercover operation since its inception. They respected each other, but no real closeness had come into being between them. Croft laid blame for that at Caliban's door. Caliban knew he was right in doing so.

'Forty-eight hours from now and it'll all be over,' Croft went on. 'Everything OK your end?' Later he would report back to his boss on what was said between them now, their last meeting before the Specials closed the net on Alvar and his associates. Closed the net? As he thought it over, Croft's mouth tightened in a grim smile, ridiculing the notion. Go in with guns at the ready and the OK to use them if necessary – that would be closer to the reality, he thought.

Caliban had been drinking his coffee when the question was put to him. Now as he replaced his cup in its saucer, 'Forty-eight more hours,' he murmured, 'and every one of them will seem like a day—'

'It'll be a bloody sight worse for Danielle,' Croft cut in. 'Who's manning her emergency call line while you're here?'

'Stewart.' But at the older man's first remark he had warmed towards him. 'I always keep my mobile phone with me, though. Just in case.'

'That ain't gonna happen, pal.' Croft saw himself as a fair mimic and he delivered this in what he considered a 'New York yob' accent.

A weird guy, this one, thought Caliban, and went back to perceiving him as a total stranger once more. 'Cut it out,' he said brusquely. 'They're ready at HQ? To move in immediately if she signals an emergency?'

'Christ, what d'you think?' Croft eyed him as if he were mentally retarded, then sipped his Bovril. 'Danielle's good,' he went on, as he put down his mug. ' "True grit", you know? As the big, slow-talking man in the film once said. If it goes sudden bad, she'll get out of there on her own, and if there's a chance in hell she'll bring with her all the stuff she's got on them.'

Caliban pushed his unfinished coffee to one side. 'Not getting anywhere, really, are we?' he said, staring down at the table.

'Seems there's nowhere to get, and I reckon that's a good sign,' Croft answered softly. 'This meet was your idea, not mine.'

'I wanted to be sure.'

'Well then, be sure.' He leaned across the table and spoke to Caliban's bent head. 'It's all set,' he said quietly. 'At 06.30 Monday morning, the Specials go in. Armed raids. At Langley Manor, to arrest Alvar. At his house in St John's Wood, to confiscate all relevant material and then to seal it off for more penetrating search. At Elena Fuentes's flat in Chelsea, to take her into custody and, as at Alvar's place, to remove relevant documents. And in Bristol at the offices and residence of Ramon Gutierrez, purposes as above. These raids are all fully co-ordinated and ready to go.'

'And Danielle runs clear of the Manor at 06.00 hours.' Caliban stood up. 'Nothing to go wrong, is there?' he said, looking down at Croft, his hooded grey eyes as ungiving as ever. 'Thanks for coming,' he added and swung away, strode out into the street.

The Special Branch man watched him go, reflecting on the fact that he had never understood why Caliban had always refused promotion. He had come to accept that he never would understand it. But he had no doubt that whatever those reasons might be they were rooted in something which had happened in Caliban's past, and that because of it he would live out his life a loner, a man abiding by a personal code burnt into his psyche deep and for ever. . . . Well, rather him than me, thought Croft, then finished his Bovril and returned to his HQ.

19

Arriving in Sutton at 5 p.m. on Saturday, Shearer booked into The Carlton, a commercial hotel on the outskirts of the town. Refusing the offer of an early call the next morning, he took the key to room 19.

'You're on the first floor,' the blonde, bored receptionist informed him. 'Up the stairs, turn right.'

Box-like in shape, purpose-furnished in the degree of comfort and quality dictated by its medium price range, his room was at the front of the hotel. Its one window offered a view across busy streets to a car-park beyond and had two armchairs placed facing it, a round table standing between them. Inspection of his small bathroom revealed it to be reasonably well equipped. Going back into the bedroom, loosening his tie as he went, Shearer unlocked his case, took out the half bottle of Glenlivet packed amongst clothing and put it on the floor. His handgun was at the bottom of the case, its silencer and a box of ammunition beside it, all padded round with flannel. He felt out the solid, meaningful shape of the gun with his hand, but did not disturb it. Then he relocked the case, put the whisky on the table, fetched the toothglass and the bottle of spring water from the bathroom, sat down and poured himself a long whisky-water.

He drank it slowly, savouring both it and the fact that once again he was on the point of direct action, that the time of preparation was over; the following day he'd take Alvar's life in payment for the evil he had done. Granted, he thought, Curtis has a point when he says that for every one I take out there's a dozen others waiting, eager and able to take his place. But he goes on to claim that I've achieved nothing of lasting value. And that's where he's wrong. Each time, I'll have achieved the death of a wrecker of other people's lives. This time, I'll kill Robert Alvar: the prospect fills me with deep satisfaction; I'll count it a useful job done well.

At the previously arranged hour of 5.45 Shearer called the number Carver had given him. It would put him in touch with Carver's mole at Langley Manor, who would report on how things stood there.

That evening he had dinner at The Carlton, then sat down to read the paper. At 9.30, to his surprise, he had a phonecall from Jack Curtis.

'You made contact with Carver's man OK?' Curtis asked.

'I did. Things appear to be developing as we thought. Danielle Fraser and Alvar arrived late yesterday afternoon. Der Broeck was already there and the three passed the evening with their hosts the de Sotos. Apart from a couple of hours this afternoon, when Alvar went out for his walk, he and the Dutchman spent today closetted together in businese discussions.'

'Fraser wasn't in on their meetings, I imagine?'

'No. She spent the afternoon strolling around the grounds or reading on the terrace.' Shearer paused a moment, and when he went on, his way of speaking, Curtis noticed, had altered. Gone was the measured impersonal tone. Listening to him, Curtis thought, he's elated, the excitement of the hunt is in him, he's seeing his hunting ground and he can hardly wait for the kill. Realizing this, Curtis was filled with horror at what was happening to this man who was his friend. 'At the front of the house a path leads from the terrace down to the woods at the bottom of the valley, goes through them and out on to the hills.' Shearer gave a small laugh. 'Alvar's been to the Manor several times before,' he said, 'and it seems he's taken that path every time he's gone out. That's what he did today, and I reckon he's ninety-nine per cent certain to do the same tomorrow afternoon; it's the only country walk of any length out from the house. But he won't be getting as far as the hills. I'll take him in the woods.'

'Maybe he won't have time for a walk tomorrow. He's down there on business.'

'He will. The mole reports Der Broeck still scheduled to leave midday Sunday, Alvar and Fraser to stay on till Monday.'

'Have you had another look at the site?'

'Don't need to. I've been there already, and I've a good memory for the location of a building and its surroundings. Besides, I've got Carver's maps. One look at them, switch on my memory, and I'm there.'

'Bully for Carver, as ever.'

Deliberately, Shearer changed the subject. 'What time's your Amsterdam flight tonight?' he asked.

'Eleven-thirty. Back on Tuesday around ten a.m.'

'Give me a ring Tuesday then.'

'I will.' Curtis hesitated, then went bull-headed at the matter which was the real point of his call. 'Drop the Alvar strike, Hal,' he said abruptly, urgently. 'Enough is enough. Drop it *now*.'

'Not a chance.' Shearer's voice was flat and cold.

And Curtis said it to him then, said the words he had resolved to say if Shearer refused to abort his killing. It cost him a lot to get them out, but he did so. 'Hal, for the record, this is the last time I'll have any part in this vendetta of yours. I'm pulling out.'

There was a longish silence. Then, 'So OK, I'll be on my own in future. Thanks for past help, Jack,' Shearer said, and cut the call.

*

Elena telephoned Michael Larman from her Chelsea flat at 10.30 on Saturday night. The call caught him unaware, angry, and somewhat depressed. The girl he had invited to his apartment had just stormed out rather drunk and saying he was shit-awful boring, had no idea what a girl really wanted on an evening out with a guy, and probably wasn't much good at providing it anyway. As soon as the door had slammed behind her he poured himself a stiff vodka and tonic and flung himself down on the sofa in the living-room to drink it and brood upon life. He sipped the vodka – then the phone rang, over on his desk by the window. Bugger you, ring on! he said to it in his mind. Then he went across and answered it. It was his aunt Elena, and he realized at once that she was in one of her ferocious tempers. They've got worse as she's got older, he reflected sourly, I'm glad she's on the other side of London right now.

But he made the right noises, offering her brief, soothingly affirmative observations whenever she paused in her vitriolic comments on the incredible beastliness of her acquaintances, the weather, prices et cetera. After all, she'd forgiven him, more or less, for the Natalie Shearer fiasco, he was thinking, only half listening to her. She'd blamed the vanished Browns for it, and he'd made no attempt to disillusion her as to his own innocence in the affair. And – so far – she had not asked for her money back.

'. . . against Shearer,' Elena said.

The name concentrated Larman's mind. 'What was that?' he said. 'Sorry, I didn't catch—'

'I said I'm going to take direct and immediate action against Shearer,' she snapped.

'But why are you so angry, my sweet Elena? All right, you're going to make a move against him. Good, if that's what you want. I just don't see why you're so worked up?'

She did not answer for a moment. Waiting, interested now, Larman guessed she was fighting for self-control. He imagined her face. It would be drained of colour, every line of it would be set hard as marble; and there would be a sort of deadness in her dark-blue eyes, a reptilian menace. He hoped she would succeed in keeping her temper. In the past he had seen her lose it, and the results had been immediate, violent and appalling. Remembering, he shuddered.

'It's Robert Alvar,' she said abruptly, harshly. 'I need his help to act against Shearer. I asked him for it again this morning. He's visiting friends down at Sutton. I rang him up there and . . . *he refused me!*'

'Surely he—'

'Robert is an arsehole! Didn't you understand what I just said? The sod refused to help me! I've given him– *Dios!* I've given him my whole life! First with Carlos, his beloved Carlos who stood surrogate for the son Robert never managed to father on his wife or any of his many mistresses. Ever since I married Carlos I've worked, lied, cheated, sometimes put my life on the line for Alvar and his fucking business – and now this!'

'But Carlos . . . I always thought that you loved Carlos? He was—'

'I *mated with* Carlos. I mated with him for the money and position it brought me. I loathed him. Loathed him, you hear? His hands on my body – ugh! – he revolted me!'

'Right from the start?'

'Right from the start!' She gave a bitter laugh. 'And I'll tell you a secret: after *the start*, it got worse. He was a pig.'

'But you had two sons by him—'

'That was part of the deal, you fool.' She laughed again; this time the laugh made Larman shiver. 'There we come to Robert again,' she went on, the words pouring out now, burning with old hatreds. 'Robert, always Robert! At first he held out against the marriage. His beloved nephew, heir-apparent to his estate – *Madre Santísima!* The wonderful Carlos could do better for himself than a Brit girl with no dowry and no useful family connections! Then, when finally he had to accept me – then, oh Christ, how Robert humiliated me! Insisted on his own doctors inspecting my body so he could be sure I was physically able to . . . ah, how shall I put it? *Serve.* Yes, able to *serve his purpose!* Then I had to sign an agreement to have at least two children by Carlos—'

'But the boys are great, Elena,' Larman interrupted, hoping to calm her. 'You love them, regardless of what Robert may say or do.'

'Love them? No. I have a blood tie to them, of course. But I don't *love* them. There's only so much love anyone has to give, you know,' she added, suddenly gone quiet. 'Everyone's capacity to love is finite.'

Larman hardly took note of her last remark at the time. He left it unexplored, unaware that it was to come back and haunt him not so very much later. 'Physical tests before marriage,' he said, 'it's no big deal, Elena, many people have them nowadays—'

'God rot the lot of them!' He had said the wrong thing and fury boiled up inside her again. 'I tell you Robert owes me! I want his help against Shearer! Robert owes me, and I'm damned well going to make him pay up!'

Larman knew something of Alvar's reputation for ruthlessness in dealing with anyone who sought to use him against his will. 'Watch it, Elena!' he cautioned her earnestly. 'You take care here!'

'*Me*, take care?' Her voice suddenly controlled and cold as death. 'No. Oh no, Michael. *He's* the one who's going to need to take care in this. You'll see. I have a plan.'

She replaced the receiver so delicately that for a moment Larman did not realize she had hung up on him. Leaving him wondering whether the 'he' she had referred to was Hal Shearer or Robert Alvar. But after a second's wondering he shrugged the whole matter away. Whichever it turned out to be, he had decided, he wasn't going to get mixed up in his aunt's machinations again. If it was Shearer she'd meant, Larman had no intention of going anywhere near the man for the rest of his life. If it was Alvar – shit, drugs barons were way out of his class!

Michael Larman settled down to a serious assault on the vodka.

20

Standing at the open window of her first-floor *en suite* bedroom at Langley Manor, dressed in her taupe business suit, Danielle leaned her forearms on the sill and looked out. It was midday, Sunday, and in ten minutes' time she must go down to the library to join Alvar. But this short while she had to herself, and the view in front of her was gorgeous: the landscaped gardens of the Manor were lovely to look upon and the sun, high in a cloudless sky, shone all their colours to brilliance. She feasted her eyes on them.

But not for long. Soon, she turned her back on the glory outside the window and went across to the desk placed against the far wall. Alvar had arranged for it to be put in her room, it was small but adequate. She sat down at it and thought through all she had done that morning, and all that remained to be done. The moment of no return was at hand: at 12.20 she would join Alvar in the library, and from then on she might have no further opportunity to correct any errors or omissions in her preparations. Therefore she now made a final check.

One: I have the three separate papers ready, giving the gist of the final agreement reached between Alvar and Der Broeck yesterday afternoon. I took it down in shorthand from Alvar last night, he instructed me to have two copies ready for him by 10.30 this morning, one for each of them, to be signed by both.

Unknown to him, I made three copies. The third one is for me and mine.

Two: Alvar told me he had taped the conversations he had with Der Broeck yesterday and this morning. I assume those tapes are in his rooms at the front of the house. Is it worth me searching for them while he's out walking this afternoon? Same answer as when I considered it before: no. I've got my high-tech recorder, I could make copies of the tapes. Too risky, though; if he caught me at it it'd blow the entire operation. So leave things be. The troops will find his tapes tomorrow morning.

Three: memo to self: remember there's still time for a cock-up! Should that occur your priority is to get out of here quick and *take with you as much spoil as you can.* As she thought that last point she smiled and got to her feet. She'd hidden the third copy she'd made of the agreement between Alvar and Der Broeck in the top drawer of her desk, beneath other papers. Now she took it out and folded it small, then unbuttoned the top buttons of her cream silk blouse and slipped the paper inside her bra. This may be an old-hat way of keeping one's secret to oneself, she thought as she did so, but it's a sure bet that where it is now it won't be discovered by accident, and if the enemy *do* discover it I'm already a goner anyway.

As she entered the library she saw Alvar on the far side of the room. He was standing with his back to her, his chin raised as he studied a picture on the wall there. 'Sorry I'm a bit late,' she said, and he turned to her.

'This meeting has been a tremendous success,' he said, advancing towards her, smiling upon her warmly. 'Thank you for all you have done.'

'I'm glad things have gone so well.' She stopped just inside the door. 'It's an advantageous deal for the consortium, isn't it? Elena will be pleased when you get back to London and tell her.'

'Elena.' His smile withered on his lips. 'Ah, Elena,' he

repeated, looking – Danielle thought – slightly shifty. 'Yes. Well, maybe the good news will improve her temper. She has been extremely difficult these last few days. Always on edge, and even more hot-tempered than usual. "Living on a short fuse": that is how Gutierrez put it before he flew back to Bristol.'

'Has Mr Der Broeck left?' Danielle had no desire to talk about Elena.

'Half an hour ago.' Alvar turned away and went across to the french doors on the far side of the room. They gave on to the terrace at the front of the house, and as he looked out he heaved a sigh of relief and pleasure, easing back his shoulders, relaxing mentally and physically. Out there in front of him he saw the path that led from the terrace down across the gardens and into the woods beyond. In his mind's eye he followed its trace through the woods and out on to the rolling hills. Not long to go now and I'll be out there, he thought. No business, no other people. Time will be mine, for the enjoying of it. Those woods down there, I will walk through them slowly, listening to birds, enjoying trees and sunshine—

'Mr Alvar, we are asked to join Mr and Mrs de Soto at 12.30 for drinks before lunch, it's time we went.'

He had forgotten his PA and his business life of which she had become such a vital part. Now her words reminded him of both – reminded him also that the de Sotos had been useful to him on many occasions in the past and might well be so again. He tore his eyes and mind away from the sunlit freedom beyond the window and went to join Danielle, thanking her for her timely reminder.

'Our hosts are going into town straight after lunch,' he went on, 'so hopefully we will not be expected to linger over coffee. I am eager to be over there on the hills.'

'Is there anything you want me to do for you while you're out?'

'Please pack up so that we are ready to leave before lunch tomorrow, I will not return to the house before five-thirty. . . .'

With Robert Alvar at her side, Danielle walked into the sitting-room at Langley Manor. The de Sotos were already there: prosperous-looking Pedro de Soto, suave, always slightly deferential towards Alvar; and his wife Conchita, a good deal younger than he, very Spanish-looking, elegantly and expensively decorative, a woman who had seldom spoken much in the company of their visitors. Danielle accepted a dry sherry from the butler and made polite conversation, wondering as she did so whether the de Sotos also would be gathered up during the police raid that would net Alvar early the following day.

That Sunday morning, Shearer had breakfast brought up to his room at The Carlton: two fried eggs, sausage, bacon, tomatoes, mushrooms, followed by toast and marmalade. Carver's telephone call came as he finished the last of the toast.

'Eleven-thirty,' Carver said. 'That car-park you can see from your room, a black Honda. I've put her over on the west side, like we said. At half-eleven I'll get out and stand beside her, keep an eye open for you. OK?'

'Right. I'll be there.'

He set out on foot from the hotel at 11.20, wearing jeans and a jungle-green bush jacket over a black T-shirt. In the top pocket of the jacket was a small pair of binoculars; in the lower right-hand pocket, a Mars bar. The loaded Mauser and its silencer were in the lower left-hand pocket and he walked with his hand inside there, curled loosely round the gun. Promptly at 11.30 he walked into the car-park and made for its far side.

Standing by the bonnet of the black Honda, Carver saw him approaching and waited where he was, a small, compactly built man with a sharp-boned face and quick, pale eyes.

'Nice-looking car,' Shearer said, running his eyes over it. 'Not too hot, I hope?'

'Snitched at the crack of dawn today. Ealing way. Owner's a single gent, departed by taxi late last night for Paris, business trip, away three days. When he gets back it'll be where he left it, like he left it.'

'Lucky guy.' Shearer got in behind the wheel, reflecting with satisfaction on his side-man's apparently unfailing ability to provide on time whatever was asked of him. He knew the secret behind that ability: Carver paid well over the odds and had never shopped anyone. Therefore he had, over the years, come to possess the confidence of a wide circle of sinners, each of whom specialized in his own favoured type of minor crime. 'Your contact at the Manor rang you?' he asked Carver as he came up at his elbow, outside the car window.

'Bang on eleven. Everything's proceeding as expected. Der Broeck was about to leave, he reported. Both the de Sotos are going into Sutton after lunch, then Alvar, his PA and the house-keeper will be the only ones left in the house until the evening staff come in at six. So good, no problems, eh? What time'll you put the Honda back?'

'Should be between five and six o'clock. But if anything queers my pitch you may have to hang about a bit.'

'No sweat. I'm a patient man.'

'One thing. About the housekeeper: where's she likely to be?'

'Seems she always spends afternoons in her rooms, it's her free time for the day. Word is she has a good snooze then, dead to the world till she goes on duty at six.'

'Sounds good. Remember now, if I don't show up by 6.30 it'll mean I'm in the shit so you get out. Scarper and stay clear, understood?'

Carver grinned, his pale eyes glinting. 'What makes you think I wouldn't? Famed far and wide for the yellow streak down my back, I am. See you.' And with an airy wave of the hand he went off towards an EXIT sign, light on his feet, quick moving.

Shearer switched on and drove out of town, taking a minor road that passed behind Langley Manor then joined up with one of the highways to the south coast. Two-miles-short of the Manor, he pulled into the small, tree-shaded layby he had used when making his earlier reconnaissance of the property. When he got out, the air was warm and a light breeze fluttered the leaves of the sycamores edging the layby. Locking the car, he climbed over the fence separating layby from pastureland and set off along the bottom of the valley, heading for the Manor. For the first hundred yards or so he was in the open and, as he walked, he scanned the hillside rising to his left. There was no one in sight. High up the slope, a little below the crest of the hill, he could see the wind-eroded knoll from whose shelter he had first sussed out the possibilities afforded by the house and its surrounding countryside. . . . No long-distance viewing for me today, he thought, as he went in amongst the trees growing on the lower slopes and along the valley floor. Today my job is hands-on and definitive.

Arriving opposite the Manor, he worked his way up to the path through the woods then padded on along it, looking about him for a suitable place to ambush Alvar. Soon, he found one. On his right, in a clearing stretching about five yards back to one side of the path, lay a massive fallen oak. During some past gale a rogue storm-wind had wrought a narrow trail of destruction through the wood at that point, and the oak was clearly the greatest of its victims. Uprooted bodily from the earth, it lay full-length on the ground, its grooved trunk bedded on branches it had crushed in its fall, its ripped-out root mass rearing skywards, a huge, solid cartwheel of dead plant growth and matted, dried soil.

That's my hide, thought Shearer. Half-a-dozen men could lie in ambush in the cover of that, let alone one. He glanced back the way he had come, then forward along the path: and he smiled in satisfaction at what he saw. For while behind him the grassy track traced a gentle curve, in front of him – the way Alvar would come from the house – it progressed in a straight line for a good twenty-five yards and then turned sharply to the right. Which meant that keeping watch on it from behind the fallen oak he would see Alvar coming in good time, and then seconds after the man had passed by he himself could step out into the open, take stance with the Mauser trained on Alvar's back and – gun him down. He would have a clear line of fire to a target he classed as being so vicious as to be beyond the protection of man's law. Perfect.

Carefully, he checked out his ambush site. He found it as well suited to his purpose as he had hoped. From one particular spot behind the trunk of the fallen oak, he would be able, using his binoculars, to keep tabs on all comings and goings on the terrace running the entire frontage of the house across the valley, therefore he would see Alvar as soon as he set out on his walk. From behind the upended root-mass of the tree, he could covertly observe Alvar as he made his way along the path towards him. And lastly, he would have no trouble in moving quietly out from hiding on to the path after Alvar had passed by, because the ground all around was covered with mosses and patches of grass, a bramble snaking here and there, twigs, but nothing to worry about providing he watched where he put his feet.

Well pleased, Shearer selected a spot affording him a clear line of vision to the terrace and leaned against the trunk of the oak to wait. Every few minutes he raised his binoculars to his eyes and studied that terrace opposite him across the valley. Even so, in a little while the quietness of the woods bore in upon his consciousness, he became aware of the serenity of the warm summer afternoon. Then he began to hear small, whispery life-sounds behind the quiet, snatches of birdsong, the fluttering of leaves as currents of air wandered through the trees, scutterings and slitherings as little creatures went about their affairs on the floor of the woods.

Straightening, he looked up at the sky. It was as blue as ever but he could no longer see the sun itself, could see only its light shimmering amongst the leaves in the higher branches of the trees. It's much the same sort of day as when I came here the first time, he thought idly – then of a sudden he stilled, his face set tight and hard. Not the same sort of day inside me, it isn't. I'm here to kill a man. A *man*? No, correction needed: Alvar's not a man, he's a raptor, a predatory creature. And one of the worst of that genus: he preys on his own kind.

Shearer focused his glasses on the Manor again. Even as he did so he saw movement at the front of the rambling old house. A man came out on to the terrace, crossed it and took the path leading down to the valley and then on through the woods to the hills beyond. Centring the binoculars on him, Shearer saw that it was Robert Alvar. Saw, too, that he was alone.

21

Driving her midnight-blue Mercedes, Elena left London for Sutton soon after midday that Sunday. Late the previous night she had decided to go down to Langley Manor and confront Robert Alvar. Her telephone call to Michael Larman, which she had made in the hope that giving vent to the anger roiling inside her would lessen its furious pressure on her emotional balance, had but served the opposite purpose. It had brought raging up, yet more violently in her blood and being, all the agonies and devastating frustrations she had suffered in the past, and by doing so had left her in the grip of a fury so intense that it had to be placated or her entire life would be empty, bereft of meaning. She *had to* bring about the death of the ex-policeman. To achieve that killing she required the assistance of Robert Alvar. Alvar had refused to give her any such help, therefore she must force him to change his mind. She could, she *would* bring him to heel. She had done so on other occasions, twice in fact. She had played the 'your grandsons are blood of your blood as they are of mine' card then, and it had worked. Provided she kept her cool, she could make it work again. Given Robert's help, I'll have Shearer dead in a fortnight, she had promised herself in the small hours of the night. And on the promise, the evil memories which had been tormenting her retreated into the dark places in her mind where they had their caves. Then good and wonderful memories had blossomed in her body and in her soul and she had slept.

Now, as she turned the Mercedes into the drive leading down to Langley Manor, a smile thinned her mouth. Yes, if I play the 'I have given you grandsons' card skilfully I'll be able to bend Robert's will to mine, I'll get my way, she was thinking. But I must keep my cool. Talk of sons and husbands can bring back despair. The black dangerous sort that storms through me like wildfire and – I'm lost then, gone feral. . . . Sometimes when that happens I can control it, but usually I can't. If it happens this afternoon, I *must* control it. I *will* control it.

The house loomed ahead as she rounded a bend, its rosy-red walls sweet in the sunlight. Turning off the drive before it swept round to the main entrance, she took the car to the rear of the building, in the hope of arriving unobserved by either Danielle Fraser or Alvar, should they be inside. Pulling up opposite the side door into the games-room she got out and walked across the paved courtyard and into the house, tall and elegant in jacket and trousers of ecru raw silk, brown-leather casuals on her feet, her blonde hair drawn back into a chignon beneath a narrow brimmed hat of supple suede. As she entered the games-room she was met by the housekeeper, Miss Keeler. A dark, thin woman, good-looking in a severe way, Miss Keeler recognized her from earlier visits and greeted her with practised ease, showing neither surprise nor curiosity although both were in her.

'I have to see Mr Alvar as soon as possible,' Elena said imperiously, after offering the bare minimum of return greetings. 'Is he in the sitting-room?'

'No, madame. He has gone for a walk. I heard him say he was going to take the terrace path, it goes—'

'I know where it goes, I went that way with him last time we were here. When did he start out?'

'It can't have been more than five minutes ago.'

'Then I'll catch him up easily. Is Fraser with him?'

'No, madame. Miss Fraser is upstairs, packing.'

'And Señor and Señora de Soto?'

'They drove into Sutton straight after lunch, madame. They are not expected back before six o'clock.'

'Good.' Impatiently, Elena made to move on past the house-keeper, only to pause and turn to her again. 'Oh, I'll be staying the night,' she said. 'My bag and suitcase are in the car, have them put in my room.'

'Madame.' Miss Keeler's black eyes met the dark-blue ones calmly. She stood straight and still until Elena Fuentes had gone out of the games-room, heading for the front of the house. 'Rich bitch and arrogant with it,' she murmured then. But in her job she had encountered Elena's type of conceit before; and having learned something of life from it she gave a wry smile and added a rider to the opinion she had just expressed. 'Rich bitch, yes, in monetary terms, but she's rotten poor as a woman,' she murmured; and went about her duties.

Having verified it was Alvar who was walking down from the Manor towards the valley bottom Shearer stood up, took his Mauser from his pocket and fitted its silencer. Then he monitored the man's progress through the binoculars, checking also that no one followed him out of the house. By the time Alvar entered the woods he had seen no one do so, therefore had decided to go ahead with his hit as planned. Thus: from behind the oak, wait for Alvar to come into sight round the bend in the straight stretch of the path; then when he's gone five or six yards beyond me, soft-foot it up to the path, set myself and – *go for it*. Put two bullets in him – check he's dead – ensure it with the *coup de grâce* if neces-sary – then get the hell out of here. Back to the car and away.

Moving alongside the fallen trunk to its exposed root-mass Shearer positioned himself behind it so that while remaining concealed, he could see the bend in the path around which Alvar would come into sight. He looked at his watch: 2.55, thirteen minutes had passed since Alvar left the house so he might come into sight any time now. He checked the Mauser, scanned his route from ambush up to the path – then as his eyes flicked back to the bend in the the track, Alvar appeared around it.

Casual-smart in brown sharkskin blouson jacket over designer chinos he was walking at an even pace, clearly enjoying himself, head up as he looked around him, following the flight of a bird through the trees or glancing at the blue ribbon of sky snaking high above him, mirror-match to the earthbound course of the path at his feet. Then as he watched the white-haired man approach, words suddenly said themselves inside Shearer's head: it could be that Robert Alvar will be my last kill. He did not *think* the augury into being, it just – was there. Instantly, savagely, he drove it out. But the words left their imprint on him; although he was not aware of it at the time, their power was on him from that moment. Unaware, he tightened his grip on the Mauser and imposed total stillness on his body, for Alvar had only a dozen more steps to take and he would draw level with the hide—

'*Robert! Wait!* I must talk to you!'

Alvar heard the woman's voice behind him. Not recognizing it, he guarded himself against possible attack, swinging round to face back the way he had come, reaching inside his jacket for the small but lethal automatic he carried with him at most times. But, even as he turned, his pursuer came hurrying around the bend in the path. Seeing it was Elena, he checked the movement before he'd touched his weapon. Furious at her intrusion he stood four-square in the middle of the path, frowning heavily.

'What brings you here?' he demanded, as she halted in front of him.

Elena resisted a desire to slap his face. 'I am sorry to break into this time you like to have for yourself,' she replied, schooling her voice and face to the expression of contrition. 'I meant to catch you before you left the house, but traffic was appalling.'

'Answer the question I asked you. I want to get on, and I don't want company.'

She drew back a little. Anger and tension were rising inside her, calling for quick release in action. Grimly, she leashed both in, telling herself she *must* keep her temper. She'd come to get from Robert Alvar *there and then* the promise of the experienced criminal help she needed, and if she antagonized him now she'd probably lose for ever any hope of getting it.

'Just before you left to come down here you told me you've arranged for me to return to South America in a fortnight's time on business for the consortium,' she said reasonably. 'That cuts short my stay over here. I'd expected longer. So I've come to ask you, again, for your help.'

'My help in what?' he snapped.

Elena gave a thin, harsh laugh at his dismissive attitude to her affairs. 'You *know* what,' she said softly. Then her chin tilted arrogantly. 'I want your hands-on assistance in putting out, and seeing through to its conclusion, a contract on the life of the man Shearer,' she went on, her voice high and clear. 'As the mother of Carlos's sons, I *demand* this favour from you!'

From the cover of the fallen oak tree, no more than twelve yards from where Elena Fuentes and Robert Alvar were confronting each other, Shearer heard her words. So he'd been right! he thought. Fuentes had somehow learnt of his killings and was out for his blood! Carefully, he crouched down behind the fallen tree and listened to what passed between them.

Elena had Alvar's full attention now. 'You *demand*? And in that tone of voice?' he enquired coldly, his dark eyes fixed on hers, hooded, opaque. 'You would do well to watch your language with me, my dear.'

My dear: the phrase warned Elena, she knew it for what it was: it was his code for 'You are living dangerously. Take care now or you will get hurt; I'll be doing the hurting myself and I'll enjoy that.' With an effort of will she looked down, biting back the fighting words rising in her throat. When a second or two later she lifted her eyes to his again they were wide and candid and her face was calm.

'I'm sorry, I wasn't thinking,' she apologized. 'I need your help, Robert. I will not be able to achieve what I have in mind without your assistance, you know that. So please, give me either Gunther Heinkel, or the American. As the mother of the two boys to whom you are happy to stand *in loco parentis*, I beg your indulgence in this.'

Such meekness of voice and manner in her first amazed Alvar, then greatly intrigued him. There must be more behind her pursuit of the man Shearer than I had realized, he thought. It all happened twenty years ago, yet *still* she will hunt him to the death! It is an obsession, truly an obsession. Yet that is not explained by the facts of the case as known to me. Therefore, I wonder, perhaps I do not know *all* those facts? Perhaps she is keeping from me certain truths, certain realities which, as the guardian of Carlos's sons, I am entitled to know? Perhaps—

'As you are aware, Elena, I shall always be grateful to you for the sons you gave Carlos,' he said, smiling briefly – and falsely – upon her. 'My only regret is that he himself is not now alive. He loved you very much.' As he spoke the last sentence he watched her closely.

'I loved Carlos with all my heart,' she said. But the fractional pause before she answered, and the sudden tension in her face, in the set of her mouth – these betrayed her.

Alvar, his perceptive, inquisitive eyes noting every subtle change in her expression, every nuance in her voice, knew her statement for a lie. Since the moment he first met her, he'd had no liking for her, and although while Carlos was still alive he had several times found himself unconvinced of the genuineness of her professed wifely love, he had for Carlos's sake kept his doubts to himself. But now, as she spoke, he felt himself set free from any obligation to 'Carlos's wife'; because, however earnestly she might declare her love for her husband, he, Alvar, was sure that *she did not love him*, that almost certainly she never had, even at the time she married him. The whore cheated Carlos, he thought, standing facing her on the path through Langley Woods, sunlight dappling the mossy grass at their feet, and now she is trying to cheat *me*. Thinks to go on trading on my love for Carlos, using the lie of loving him to win my help in her private act of vengeance against the ex-policeman who—

'I have yet to understand, Elena, the intensity of your desire to have this fellow Shearer killed,' he said. 'It was so long ago. This causes me to wonder ... was there perhaps something more between you and him? Something sexual? You had an affair with him, and he jilted you?'

For a moment he thought she was going to spit in his face. Then she controlled herself. 'Loved – *Shearer*?' Her voice was steady but there was no natural colour left in her cheeks; her skin had gone white beneath her make-up. 'I hate him,' she said, a kind of deadness in her voice. 'I think once I have killed him I shall wish I could bring him back to life so that I could have the pleasure of killing him again.'

For a second, Alvar felt himself in the presence of evil and his scalp crawled. Then the frisson passed and a prurient and sadistic excitement coursed through him. There is indeed something to be discovered here, he thought. I have observed a great deal of hatred in my time but the hatred consuming Elena as we stand here is unlike anything I have met before, it is altogether more complex, a deeper, an almost elemental emotion. Also, it is something she has always kept secret, kept for herself alone. So,

now I will take it from her. It will be like raping a virgin but –
more so, because—

'For God's sake, Robert!' she cried. 'Just promise me one of the
men and the back-up they'll need to do the job, that's all I'm
asking!'

'What *is* Shearer to you?' he persisted, intent on ravishing her.

Colour flared the ashen cheeks. Her strong, long-fingered
hands clenched into fists. 'He's the murderer of *my brother!* He
killed James. You know that, you've known it ever since you've
known me, I've made no secret of it!'

'That was twenty years ago, and you gun for him now?
Besides, he shot James Smith in the line of duty. Your beloved
brother James was a petty criminal, a drug pusher and not a very
clever one at that—'

'*Shut your fucking mouth!*' Her face convulsed with fury, Elena
crammed down the rage inside her – and with it went all
thought of her vengeance on Shearer, and of the favour she had
followed Alvar to demand or cajole from him. Body and soul,
she was with James Smith, her brother. 'What do you know of
James?' she went on, an exaltation flaming her face. '*My beloved
brother*, as you just referred to him. You were being sarcastic, of
course,' – she moved a step closer to Alvar, never taking her eyes
off his – 'but, d'you know, you spoke no less than the truth when
you said that. He *was* my brother, and he *was* my beloved.'

Alvar's face froze. 'No, Elena,' he said, tight-lipped. 'You
never loved any man in your life. The capacity for the true self-
abandon of sexual passion is not in you. You're frigid. Carlos
told me.'

'*Carlos* told you that?' She laughed in his face. 'Carlos's love-
making was all ardent gestures but little performance,' she
jeered. 'After James, he was—' The laugh was cut off abruptly,
and she leaned towards Alvar. 'After James, Carlos was a nothing, a puling, pathetic nothing of a man,' she said.

'And your brother was a common roughneck, an errand-boy shot dead in a London alleyway.'

'Didn't stop me loving him!' Elena could feel the unforgettable passion rising inside her, storming through her in the pulsing of her blood. 'James and I, we loved each other body and soul and we gave both of those full rein. It was marvellous with him, living life with him – making *love* with him!'

'But the only children you gave birth to out of your body grew there from the seed of Carlos!' Alvar was seeking to cut the heart out of the love which had existed between her and her brother and still held her enthralled, for to do so seemed to him the only way of preserving Carlos's honour – and therefore his own. 'Wasn't James *man enough* to achieve that?' he taunted her. 'Perhaps he was impotent—'

'*You shit!*' Elena sprang at him like a striking cat, taloned fingers crooked to rake across his cheeks. But she was not quite fast enough. Alvar's reflexes were quicker still. He took a half-step back, braced himself, then as she struck at his face he grabbed her right forearm just above the wrist with one hand, knocked her left arm off its line of attack with an upward sweep of the other and pushed her savagely away from him. Her hat went flying, she stumbled back and stood with her head down, breathing heavily, glaring across at him up-from-under, her eyes fey. Memories of her lost, too well-remembered love were flowing in her hot and free. Then suddenly they laid torch to her long-repressed lust to exact payment for past agonies endured – and she turned rabid wild.

She hurled herself at him, got right in close before he'd realized her intention, raked her nails across his jawline then brought up her right leg and kneed him in the groin. Alvar had seen it coming and twisted his body sideways; he took it half on his upper thigh, half on his genitalia. Gasping and grunting with pain he bent over double, arms clasped across his belly. Elena beat at his arched back with her fists and kicked at his legs, hurling obscenities at him as she did so, curses in English and Spanish pouring out of her spitting mouth in a vicious, triumphant monotone.

Alvar kept his head down, taking the punishment, grinding his teeth in fury and agony. But he was biding his time. And as soon as he'd mastered the pain he slid his right hand inside his jacket as he'd done once before that afternoon – but this time his hand closed round the butt of his small but lethal handgun. Then judging his moment, he dodged a kick and straightened up to face her, pulling out the weapon, pointing it at her heart.

'Get back! Get away from me, *you incestuous slut!*' he snarled.

It was one word that stopped her. '*Incestuous?*' Her arms fell to her sides, she took a step back and stood, still and straight, blonde hair tumbled down over her shoulders. Then she smiled, but not at Alvar although she was looking in his direction. 'There was love between me and James,' she said quietly. 'Whatever adjective you put with it doesn't really matter. It doesn't alter the fact of the love.'

'You disgust me! You and your brother, you are scum, you are filthy—'

Her face contorted and she flung herself at him again. He wasn't ready for it. It simply hadn't occurred to him she might not be held in check by the threat of the gun and now she grappled with him, grabbing for his weapon.

He stood firm against her, and they locked together in a ferocious struggle for possession. Alvar was physically the stronger, but Elena's body was powered by the wild elation coursing through her. She was fighting for the only thing in her life that had ever really mattered to her. To overcome Alvar would be to proclaim and validate the worth, the excellence of what she and her brother had lived together, and for that she strove against Robert Alvar with all that was in her.

But the battle was shockingly brief. Alvar had turned the barrel of his gun aside as she slammed into him, and now her body pinned his arm and weapon against his chest. He tried to throw her off. She resisted, hooking her left arm around his neck then bringing her right up to join it – her two hands encircled his neck and she rammed the balls of her thumbs against his windpipe, seeking to cut off his breathing, all the time keeping her body pressed tight against his. To her at that moment it seemed that the pain she had lived in since her brother's death could be exorcised by the one simple act only: *kill*. Just *do it*; you'll be quiet inside yourself after that.

As her strangle-hold on his neck tightened, Alvar felt the touch of death on him and realized that his only hope was to get his gun free and *use it*. He must disable this harpy at his throat – put a slug in her shoulder, that'd get her off him. Frantically, he intensified his efforts to wrench his right arm free so that he could use the weapon. He had it nearly clear when she sensed the threat. 'No, you don't!' she gasped, and grabbed blindly for the gun. Her hand closed around his where it grasped the butt, for one second they struggled – then the gun went off! And fired again!

Two shots, the reports muffled by their bodies. Then Alvar saw *and felt* Elena die. She shuddered as the bullets cut through flesh to her heart and lungs, then her head lolled back, her chin pointing at the sky, mouth falling open in the rictus of mortal shock, tousled blonde hair sliding back from her face. Her legs gave way and she slumped to the ground, lay sprawled at his feet. And through a lifetime of ten seconds Alvar stood rigid, looking down at her, his mind a blank. Then he became aware of the presence of woodland all around him, a warm and sunbright greenness – heard again the lively calls of birds amongst the trees – *and realized he was still holding the gun.*

At once his mind cleared of everything except the imperative need to take steps to ensure that he himself should come out of this disaster as being guiltless before the law. Before the law: that was the factor which mattered, it was all that mattered. He was no stranger to breaking the law, but so far in his life he had never been proven guilty of any crime although he had connived at, organized or committed many. Almost immediately he decided that by far the most promising way of continuing that state of affairs in this present situation would be to make Elena's death look like a suicide. The gun was his, but no one other than Danielle Fraser and his security chief down in Bristol knew that, the man had got it for his boss himself. So now, Alvar reasoned, standing stock still in a patch of sunlight in Langley Woods, now he should check a) that Elena was actually dead; b) the angle of the entry wounds in relation to c) the position in which the body was lying, so that if necessary he could alter that to conform with b). He knew for a fact that women suicides very seldom shot themselves in the head.

Slipping his gun back into its shoulder harness under his jacket he knelt beside her. Blood had trickled from her nose and mouth, he noticed, also—

'Raise both hands above your head, Alvar!' The male voice struck at him from the other side of Elena's body and in reflex reaction to the shock of it, his head and hands lifted on the instant. He saw that the man facing him from a few yards away had him at gunpoint, the handgun gripped in those clasped hands was trained on his heart. 'Now get on your feet.'

Awkwardly, Alvar obeyed, eyes riveted on his new and suddenly arrived enemy. He did not recognize him. He saw a tall, well-built man; the eyes were piercing, the facial bones strong, the hair straight and dark: no, it was not a face he knew. Was there any chance the man might be bought? he wondered desperately. In his experience most men had their price, provided you could pay it – and he most likely could.

'Who are you?' he asked, already feeling more confident.

His captor walked towards him, halted six feet from Elena's body. Alvar could see his eyes properly now, and his budding confidence withered and died, vanished without trace; for on closer viewing he did not think this was a man likely to perjure himself for cash payment.

'Does it matter who I am?' The eyes behind the gun were grey.

'You called me by my name, so I thought we might . . . talk.'

A faint smile twisted the long, thin mouth. 'My name is Shearer,' he answered. 'What do you think you and I should talk about, Roberto Alvarez?'

22

Immediately after lunch, Danielle went up to her bedroom on the first floor and changed into jeans and green linen overblouse, slipped bare feet into leather sandals, then cleared her desk, stowing the files and equipment required for Alvar's meeting with Der Broeck back into the 'office' briefcase in which they had been brought down. That done, she unlocked and part-packed her own suitcase, leaving out clothes and accessories she would yet need. Her mobile phone she left where it was at the bottom of the case, swaddled in a cream cashmere sweater. She thought of that phone as her lifeline to the outside world, for she had only to tap out the emergency number and say 'Touchstone, scramble' and out there the entire operation would be ratcheted up to whatever red-alert action the situation required at the time.

Relocking the case she went across to the open window and stood looking out. Before her eyes Langley Manor's gardens glowed beneath the sun, but she wasn't seeing them. Inside her head the facts and times of her plans burned yet more brilliantly. She checked through them. At 6.00 tomorrow morning I walk out of this place, the weather men forecast a perfect day so should I encounter house-staff I say I'm having a stroll before breakfast. I go down through the gardens at the front, then, as soon as I'm out of sight of the house, I cut back to the drive, go up it to the road, turn left and walk along the straight stretch there. A quarter-mile on I'll see a blue Ford Escort parked on the verge. Its driver will look as though he's just finished changing the back wheel, but actually he'll be waiting for me to turn up so – we get in and drive off. Then at 6.30 the Specials move in on their four separate targets: on the Manor, on Alvar's house in St John's Wood, on Fuente's flat in Chelsea, and on Gurierrez's set-up in Bristol—

Abruptly, a shiver coursed through her and she shut her eyes, clenched her teeth, compressed her lips. Success is close, yes, she thought, but they say the closing hours of a long operation are the most dangerous of all. Well, they've arrived – and what if something goes wrong now? I could be trapped here at Alvar's mercy—

Shit, woman, get a grip on yourself! Exerting her will she fought clear of her momentary loss of nerve. Then she got on with living out those 'closing hours' as if they were but ordinary hours in the pattern of her working day.

Seeing from her watch that it was nearly 3.15, she knew she had more than two hours to fill before Alvar got back from his walk. Deciding to spend the time reading on the terrace she picked up sunglasses and the illustrated copy of *Gulliver's Travels* she had discovered in the de Sotos' library and went downstairs. As she reached the bottom of the main staircase and was about to step into the hall, the housekeeper emerged from the corridor on her right and made for the stairs. She was carrying a vase of crimson roses in her hand.

'Madame Fuentes arrived a little while ago,' Miss Keeler said, pausing beside Danielle. 'She will stay the night so I am getting her room ready.'

'Oh?' Danielle contrived a note of mildly interested surprise, but the news awoke in her a flicker of apprehension that Elena's arrival at the Manor might signal some threat to Special Branch's operation. 'I didn't know she was expected,' she said.

'Señora de Soto didn't advise me of it.'

'So she will have a pleasant surprise when she returns from Sutton.' But this 'kite' remark elicited no response other than an enigmatic smile, and her unease increased. Because what had Fuentes come here *for*? Was it possible she had somehow got wind of the op. and had come to warn Alvar? Had she— 'I'll go and see if I can be of any assistance to Madame Fuentes,' Danielle announced crisply. 'Is she in her room?'

Miss Keeler observed the sudden assumption of authority, and her interest in the present goings-on of the guests at the Manor increased. Her face, however, showed no sign of it. 'No, Miss Fraser,' she answered. 'Madame Fuentes said she wanted to see Mr Alvar as soon as possible. When I told her he'd gone out on his walk she said she would follow and catch him up.'

'She knows the walk through the woods and on to the hills?'

'Of course, from previous visits. Mister Alvar only set out about five minutes before she arrived, she'll soon catch him up.' Then Miss Keeler smiled her narrow, buttoned-up smile and went on her way up the stairs.

Frowning, Danielle went out on to the terrace and sat down in a beechwood chair, her back to the sun. Opening her book at random she found herself looking at a full-page illustration of Gulliver being staked out for safe-keeping by his Lilliputian captors. The drawing was beautifully executed and full of interest, but two seconds later her eyes were on the woods across the valley. The scenario re Alvar had changed – and changed in a way which filled her with foreboding. Alvar will be enjoying his walk over there in the woods, she thought, Fuentes will catch him up then presumably they'll go on together. But why has she come? What can have happened? What can possibly be so urgent that she couldn't use the phone or wait until Alvar returns to London? And what shall I do now? Does the event warrant action? Shall I use my emergency mobile phone and inform Caliban?

Two reports cracked the sunlit country peace across, and across again – *gunshots!* Oddly muffled in sound but – *gunshots!* Danielle leapt to her feet and stood staring across at the wooded slopes rising from the valley floor in front of her. That was where the shots had come from, over there up in the woods. Two shots, close together. And Alvar was in those woods, so was Fuentes. Dear God! What had happened? What *was happening*, maybe, even as she stood listening? Should she dash into the house to summon help? she wondered, then immediately dismissed the idea, deciding it would be best to play this alone, providing she got the chance to. Best to discover for herself exactly what had come to pass over there, then play the hand dealt her by that discovery in whatever way she judged likely to avert any disruption whatsoever of the imminent strike against Alvar and his associates. That operation *must not* be put in jeopardy.

A quick survey of the house showed it basking in the sunshine undisturbed by either sound or movement within it. Convinced that she alone had heard the shots she sped off the terrace at a run, dark hair flying behind her, sandalled feet swift across grass. But before she had gone twenty yards – a third shot cracked the quiet! Immediately she froze, listening. Heard only ... silence ... and her own breathing behind it, fast, uneven. And while she listened, her trained mind went its own way, recording known facts. Three shots so far. Two first, slightly muffled and in close succession to each other. Then a pause lasting two or three minutes, then ... a third shot. And all were fired from the same gun. Fact? Yes, fact. ... Then awakened instinct strung those facts together and slapped their warning corollary to the forefront of her mind: *whoever's got that gun is still in the woods ahead of you.* Alvar? Or Fuentes? Immaterial – neither will be friend to you in this! Neither can afford to be, in the circumstances. So go on now, but proceed circumspectly. You need to see which of them it is who's in there with the gun *before they see you*. Your life may depend on it.

Therefore, Danielle moved off the path and went on to the valley bottom still swiftly but now with a certain care, keeping in by the massed rhododendrons and syringas bordering it. Then she made her way leftwards alongside the hedge fringing the woods, and rejoined the path where it led in under the trees.

From bright sunshine into the light-and-shade world of the greenwood: as she went in under the oaks and sycamores she at once felt safer. Keeping to the side of the track, flitting along parallel to it and making use of all available cover in the form of treetrunks, bushes and undergrowth, she shadowed the way Alvar had said he would take on his walk. Dead leaves, moss and thin grass cushioned her footfalls. One part of her mind was clamouring hurry, hurry! Someone up there ahead of you may need life-or-death help so – *hurry!* But she was heeding the other, professional part which said, make too much noise and whoever's got the gun now will hear you coming and – well, you won't be much use to anyone if you're dead, will you?

With this in mind she went on in stops and starts, light-footed, hawk-eyed for human form or movement ahead of her on the path. As the moments passed, the quietness of the woods seemed to her to become more oppressive. Once, a flurry of bird-calls showered across it; they died their separate deaths quickly, ghosted the leafy corridors of the woods for an atom of time and then were gone. As the quietness closed around her again Danielle saw that a short distance in front of her the path turned sharply to the left. She halted, took cover behind a treetrunk and peered round it at the bend before her. Surely, she thought, she must by now be close to – whatever it was she was going to find? The shots had seemed to come from fairly close to where the path entered the woods. Get beyond that corner, then surely she'd know? She'd *see*?

So *move!* snapped a voice inside her head, and she darted out on to the path and sped on. Feet quick-quiet over the long-dead flowers of celandines she reached the bend, rounded it and – froze. The shock of what she saw was instant, terrifying and, for a split second, totally paralysing. Then she raced on towards the two bodies sprawled on the path, no more than twenty yards apart from each other. Came to Robert Alvar first, stood looking down at him. He was dead. He had to be, the right side of his face and head was blown away. His body lay on its back, left shoulder at an unnatural angle, clothing dishevelled and spattered with blood. His right arm was stretched out sideways, his hand lay lax on the ground there and both it and the gun loosely held in it were drenched with brain tissue and gore.

As Danielle stared down at the weapon, four or five ants appeared at the edge of the pooled blood fouling the earth beneath and around it and began to investigate the shape and nature of this strange substance so suddenly discovered in their habitat. Their darting, purposeful movements caught her eye. She watched, fascinated, while in obedience to some primeval call sent out by these outriders of the tribe, more and more ants appeared from various directions, a growing horde of tiny brown bodies scurrying hither and thither, each intent on its own task yet the company mysteriously seeming to work as one—

Ants? Ah Christ! What *are* you thinking of, woman? With a strangled sob Danielle shuddered, jerked her head aside and ran on along the path to where Elena Fuentes lay. She'd known in the half-second she'd stood shock-paralysed on her first sight of the bodies that the far one was Elena's: a woman's clothes, and blonde hair spilling across the thin grass. Now she knelt beside her. Here, there was none of the stark, obscene horror of Alvar's death. Elena lay on her side in a position almost foetal, bent knees drawn up towards her chest; her right arm was hugged tightly in against her stomach, the left was splayed across her face, half-covering it. At first glance she looked as though she was perhaps sleeping. Then the blood-soaked raw silk covering her right arm and the front of her body told the truth: Elena also was dead.

As this second hard fact registered in her brain, Danielle closed her mind against everything except the urgent need to place the two fatalities in the context of the impending and complex Special Forces operations against Alvar and his consortium – and then to take immediate steps to ensure that those operations went forward to the best possible advantage in the new circumstances. Which meant – didn't it? – that the raids on the respective properties of Elena and Alvar, plus the arrest of Gutierrez in Bristol, must be carried out with all speed. Once the deaths were discovered and news of them got into the public domain – which could not be delayed for long now – it would be likely to reach Alvar's associates, whereupon they would assuredly take swift action to have incriminating evidence and documents destroyed or removed from their bosses' offices. She herself, therefore, must now ascertain and commit to memory, rapidly and as far as possible without disturbance to the crime scene, all facts relevant to the killings: calibre and make of gun, particulars of wounds, position of bodies in relation to one another, signs – if any – of struggle. After that she must return to the Manor and – and do what? Which of her two undoubted duties should she carry out first on arriving back there?

She answered her own question almost at once: as soon as I've taken note of the details of what's happened here I must get up to my room unobserved, use my mobile phone *and report in to Caliban.* Given any sort of luck I'll be able to do that. But if I meet anyone before I can, I'll have to bow to the inevitable, have to ring the local police and call them out to the house.

Seven minutes later, she started back through the birdsong woods. As she ran she was willing, *praying* for luck to stay with her just that bit longer – long enough for her to make her call.

'Red. Oberon calling Caliban. Red.'

'Hang on. May take a sec., just hang on.'

'Will do.' Hurry, hurry, *hurry*—

'Caliban. Speak.'

Danielle gave him the facts cold: Fuentes and Alvar were dead, lay dead of gunshot wounds in Langley Woods. She had heard the shots from the terrace, gone to investigate, found the bodies. So far as she could tell, no one else was as yet aware of the deaths.

'How many shots?' he asked.

'Three. Two in close succession, followed by an interval of three minutes or so, then the third.'

'All from the same gun?'

'Beyond a shadow of doubt.'

'Wounds?'

'Alvar, gun muzzle to his right ear. Messy. Fuentes, shot through the chest and abdomen at close quarters, *very close* quarters.'

'What's your thinking on it?'

'What's there on scene *suggests* the following events. There was a struggle between the two of them for possession of the gun. In the course of it the gun was fired twice and Fuentes was shot dead. Whereupon Alvar, horrified at what would probably be accounted murder, with himself cast as murderer, committed suicide.'

'You emphasize *suggests*. Which means you think – what? That someone else was involved? A third person was present?'

'It's more . . . well, Alvar's not *like* that! Suicide – it's not in his mindset!' This burst out of her, a conviction born of knowing the man, of working closely with him for over two years. Then she added slowly, as though puzzled by her own uncertainty, her suspicions in the matter, 'Besides, it didn't . . . it didn't feel right.'

'OK, but we'll leave all that till later.'

Standing by the wash-basin in her bathroom, mobile phone held to mouth and ear, Danielle heard the impatience in his voice, frowned resentfully, then accepted that he was right and forced her mind back to the present crisis.

'Here's how we play this from now,' Caliban went on. 'You're ready to move out at once?'

'Yes. Provided you're moving in to take over.'

'Given you're right and no one else heard the shots, how long before anyone at the Manor's likely to get curious when Alvar doesn't return there? To the extent of going out to look for him?'

'You've got until about five-thirty, I'd say, given no one else heard the shots – and if they *did* hear them they'd probably be out and about by now, but there's no one around far as I can tell. The de Sotos aren't expected back before six. House staff come in again at five-thirty. The housekeeper's in, but she always keeps to her rooms from three to six.'

'Good. So you get out of there soon as this call's finished. Proceed exactly as was planned for tomorrow; if the bloke with the car isn't in place by the time you get there, you wait in cover for him to show up, he'll not be long.'

'Just – go?' It seemed too . . . too easy. Just to walk away, and Alvar and Fuentes lying dead in the woods across the valley.

'All your records on Alvar and co., they're in your room, locked up?'

'Yes – the Der Broeck stuff, that is. The rest is in my room at the St John's Wood house, not much, you've had most of it.'

'So do like I said!' But he had sensed her disorientation, and softened his tone. 'The driver, he'll be in place in twenty minutes' time – not the chap who was on the job originally, I'll co-opt someone from the Sutton force.'

Angry with herself that he'd thought the soothing touch necessary, she asked sharply, 'How're you going to deal with this?'

'Two parts to it. First part, I ensure that your local police present themselves at Langley Manor within half an hour at the most; that they will be accompanied by half-a-dozen Special Branch men already in Sutton for the action scheduled for tomorrow; and that the investigation into the two deaths, together with all tangential matters he may consider relevant – which remit will cover practically everything he wants, of course – will be at the discretion and command of the senior Special Branch officer present.'

'Who, I assume, will be very senior indeed?'

'He will. My second move will be to contact London HQ, apprise them of the present state of play, and recommend that the raids on Alvar's house in St John's Wood, Fuentes's flat in Chelsea, and Gutierrez's place in Bristol all be advanced to GO immediately.'

'Sounds good.'

'Then I'll get at it. Good luck – oh, wait! Will you do something for me?'

'Name it.'

'Before I contact you again, think back to that crime scene in the woods and clarify in your mind everything about it, get your memory of it clear and detailed. I'll be wanting to plunder those recollections as soon as I've got the time. Including, please, that *feel* you mentioned.'

'That a third person might have been present, you mean?'

'I gathered the possibility occurred to you?'

'Yes, it did.' Then at once her thoughts arrowed away from Caliban and the operation so suddenly thrown into emergency gear by events. Instead they fastened, fascinated, on the perhaps illusory figure of a possible 'third man' in close proximity when Alvar and Fuentes met their deaths. . . .

'So *think on it*,' Caliban said. 'We'll get back to it later. Out. Out now.'

23

Jack Curtis arrived back in London from Amsterdam on Tuesday morning and went straight to his office. There he quickly became aware that the anti-narcotics fraternity was, and had been since Sunday evening, in a state of euphoria and hyperactivity. On discovering the reasons for this he went to work at once to find out everything he could about what had taken place. By the time he had pieced the story together, and explored certain aspects of it in depth, he knew he had to do two things: he must acquaint Hal Shearer with all he'd just learned; and somehow he must ensure that Hal met the woman whose special knowledge of the matter could easily be a threat to him – potentially a devastating threat.

But on telephoning Shearer's office, he was informed that he was not expected in at all that day, but had left a message asking Curtis to call round at the Heathrow apartment any time after six o'clock that evening. He did so, ringing the doorbell at five minutes past the hour.

'Have a successful trip?' Shearer asked, as he led the way into the sitting-room and set about pouring drinks.

'Christ, Hal, you were lucky you weren't caught this time!' Curtis flung himself down in the large, leather-upholstered armchair that was his favourite. 'If narcotics had been running tight surveillance on Langley Manor on Sunday, they'd have nicked you—'

'From what I've gleaned from the papers, I'm surprised they hadn't got the place staked out.' Shearer handed him a glass of whisky and water, sipped his own, and stood looking down at him. 'D'you know why they hadn't?'

'That's quite a story. And it's one I've only just heard.'

'Tell me.'

'In a while.' Curtis looked up at him. 'Did you kill Alvar?' he asked.

Shearer turned away and sat down facing him, put his glass on the side table at his elbow and stared at him. 'What do you think?' he asked coldly.

So Curtis changed tack, thinking, if you're going to stonewall I'll mosey in on you from the side and then – bloody well take stance beside you against all-comers, should that turn out to be necessary.

'At this moment, all I'm thinking is that you'd probably be interested to hear a run-down of official thinking on the killings,' he said.

For a moment Shearer's eyes held his, brooding, guarded; then suddenly he smiled. 'Thanks,' he murmured.

The account Curtis gave was concise but detailed; Shearer listened closely and made no comment until it was finished. When it was, he sat forward and spoke. 'So it seems the media's dramatic inferences and assumptions as to what actually happened in the woods at Langley Manor have been borne out by better informed, professional investigation,' he said. 'In short, that the gun belonged to Alvar, he and Fuentes quarrelled, he drew his gun, they fought for possession of it and, as they did so, it was fired and Fuentes fell dead. Filled with guilt and remorse, Alvar then blew his brains out. . . . Sensitive guy, wasn't he,' he added drily.

'You don't go along with the suicide bit, I gather. In that you share the opinion of the first person to arrive on the scene, Danielle Fraser. Her off-the-record opinion, that is. Publicly she voices the official line.'

'I saw references to Fraser in the papers.' Shearer's voice was casual, but he looked away from Curtis because it had come as a considerable shock to him to learn that Alvar's PA questioned – even off the record – the theory that his death was suicide. 'They didn't say much about her personally. No pictures, only the vaguest description.'

'Her real name's Caine, Justine Caine,' Curtis said.

'*Real* name? Why the alias, I wonder? Skeleton in the family? Or maybe for cosmetic purposes? "Justine Caine". It lacks. . . .' He paused. 'Myself, I don't think it lacks anything,' he said.

'Neither does the woman herself lack anything. Caine's a policewoman. She's been working undercover for the last two years and more as PA to Alvar.'

'*What?*' Shearer was on his feet, narrowed eyes fixed on Curtis. 'She's with the Specials? A career officer with the Specials? She was informing on Alvar all that time?'

'Just so. It was one big op., Hal. Started up two and a half years ago, ran deep and wide. And, by God, they made a good job of keeping it under wraps. All that time, and I didn't get a whiff of it – first I heard was when I got back from Amsterdam this morning.'

While Curtis was speaking, Shearer padded across to the window and stood gazing out at an area of parkland below him, hands in the pockets of his trousers, his back to the room. As he listened, he was thinking about Danielle Fraser, alias Justine Caine – no, the other way round, actually, wasn't it? So, she wasn't after all simply Alvar's PA! She was a highly trained policewoman, it was *she* who had found Alvar and Fuentes dead, and according to Curtis she had, thus far off-the-record, reservations as to the acceptability of the suicide theory to account for Alvar's death. *So what hypothesis did she postulate in its place?*

'Caine was manoeuvred into position,' Curtis said. 'The Specials ran an "arranged" raid on a drugs deal involving some of Alvar's underlings down in Bristol. She was already infiltrated there, in a minor way. During that raid she got one of the villains safely out and away, whereupon Alvar looked upon her with great favour and gave her the PA job, shifting the incumbent to Gutierrez at his HQ. It was owing to the information she – and others too, of course – supplied that Special Branch was able to plan those co-ordinated strikes on the consortium's top guns. The killings at the Manor nearly wrecked the whole thing, but some pretty quick action saved the day, thank God.'

'Quick action by who?'

Curtis smiled broadly. 'Caine. She got back to the house unobserved and rang in to her emergency contact. He passed it on but fast, the earth moved and – presto! The consortium got hammered!'

Turning, Shearer leaned back against the window ledge. 'You seem to know a lot about all this, although it's not your field,' he said. 'How come?'

'You know how. In the past you've profited from it – if that's the right word – yourself. My job allows me access to certain information, and *sources* of information.'

'Up to a certain level.'

'Correct. Levels which, as you well know, I have sometimes . . . successfully ignored.'

'You've gone out on a limb for me before. Is that what you're considering doing here?'

Curtis thought for a moment, frowning. Then his face cleared and he grinned across at Shearer. 'Hell, man, quit mucking about,' he said. 'Why not ask me straight out?'

'Ask you what?'

'If I think you shot Alvar dead.'

'All right. Do you?'

'I haven't decided.' The grin was gone from Curtis's face, it might never have been. 'Hal, come and sit down again,' he said. 'It's not important to me whether you did or didn't, as you should know by now. What is important is that I don't want to see you jailed for it.'

Shearer regarded him in silence for a full minute, then went back to his chair and sat down. 'Correct me if I'm wrong,' he said, 'but it occurs to me we both think it's possible that Justine Caine suspects a third person was on scene when Alvar and Fuentes died.'

'No correction needed.'

'Has that premise occurred to anyone *else*, d'you know? Anyone Caine might have reported to? Anyone sufficiently high up and with official interest in the case?'

Curtis shook his head. 'I thought about that, and decided it hasn't. If it had, I'd have got a whisper of it.'

'Have you met Caine?'

'Twice. A quiet personality, very efficient, rather reserved, I'd say.' He smiled. 'Very attractive, too,' he added.

'I know. Though I hardly saw her face.' And as he spoke, clear inside Shearer's head came a picture of Justine Caine as he'd seen her that night in Barcelona earlier in the year when he'd watched her come out of the Meridien hotel and join Alvar. She'd walked away with him – 'Danielle Fraser', his PA – and . . . yes, there'd been a subtle, lissom fluency in the way she moved – a personal magnetism – which had held him spellbound; he'd watched her until night and distance had stolen her from him. 'Is she married?' he asked.

Curtis stared at him, then sipped his whisky and put the glass down. 'She was,' he answered. 'To a businessman, some highflyer in the City. She divorced him years ago. No children. Is that enough for you?'

'Do you know any more?'

'Some.' Curtis had been studying Shearer's face, but he had not learned much from it. Him and Justine Caine, they're two of a kind, he thought, neither go through life wearing their hearts on their sleeves. And in his mind he wished them joy of each other. Then he went on to tell Shearer more about her. 'Her parents were killed in a plane crash when she was eleven. She and her brother, the only kids, were brought up by a maiden aunt. From what I gather, they both tend to be loners. They're close to each other, though; always have been, I understand. They're in the same trade – he was her contact man all through the Alvar operation. On the job, he's a cracker. A handsome bastard, too. Know what? His code name for the Alvar op. was Caliban – and it was she who put it on him.'

To Curtis's surprise, Shearer smiled. 'What was hers?' he asked.

'Oberon. . . . Why the interest, Hal?'

'I'd like to meet her.' He frowned, corrected himself at once. 'No! To hell with that! I've *got to* meet her! You've just told me she's a highly trained and experienced policewoman. She must know what she's looking for at the scene of a crime. If she *does* suspect a third person was present when the killings took place she'll have her reasons for it, she'll have *evidence*, presumably! If she has, I could find myself in serious trouble.'

'*If*. Big little word—'

'I must meet her, Jack. Any idea how?'

Earlier that day Curtis also had come to the conclusion that it would be useful – essential, even! – for the two to meet, and he had taken steps to make that possible. Now he sat back in his chair, smiling.

Shearer caught the movement. 'You've thought of something?' he demanded hopefully.

'Odd, how things work out, isn't it?' Curtis murmured. Then he got to work. 'How are you fixed for Thursday evening?' he asked. 'Are you available?'

'You set me up a meeting with Caine and I'll be there!'

'Not so fast!' Curtis was still smiling. 'What I've set up is a social occasion, not a briefing! You'll have to put on the charm – you're not a bad hand at that when you put your mind to it.'

'What's the occasion?'

For answer, Curtis took a white, unsealed envelope from the pocket of his jacket, got up and gave it to him. Shearer opened it and drew out the pasteboard card inside. It was an invitation to drinks and buffet supper at Curtis's house in Thornton Heath the coming Thursday evening, eight o'clock onwards.

'Big do?' he asked, looking up.

'Around twenty. Mostly from the office, but there'll be others too, neighbours.'

'She'll be there? Caine?'

'She will.'

'Who's she coming with?'

'Herself, I understand. She knows some of the office lot, of course.'

24

Shearer arrived at the Thornton Heath house on Thursday evening to find Curtis's sister Ann hostessing his party for him. A sophisticated and attractive woman, divorced five years earlier on account of her inattention to her marriage caused by her near total commitment to her high-powered media job, she opened her brother's front door to him, welcomed him with practised warmth then led him into the sitting-room. Half-a-dozen men and women were grouped in there, drinking and partying, but its sliding glass doors stood open to the patio beyond and other guests were out there in the cool evening sunshine. Ann stopped at the table just inside the door and, while a hired barman prepared the whisky sour Shearer asked for, asked him if he would like to be introduced to Justine Caine straightaway.

'Jack told me you wanted to meet her,' she went on, as he took his drink and the two of them strolled towards the sliding doors. 'She's out on the patio. The dark-haired woman in the sea-green dress standing facing us, listening to the tall, thin, blond young man with heavy spectacles. See? He's probably boring her out of her head, he talks computers all the time. Shall we go over?'

Shearer had indeed seen her. And on the instant, that same intense sense of awareness of her as had suffused him when he'd seen her for the first time – a sort of recognition of her self, her

special being – flooded through him again. As it did so he realized he needed a little time before he met her otherwise he
would quite possibly be too . . . too open to her? 'Thanks, Ann,
but not to bother,' he said. 'You take off now, I'm at home here,
you know that, and I see several people I'd like a chat with. I'll
introduce myself to Miss Caine later on.'

But when Ann left him he did not at once go to talk with any
of those acquaintances of his who were present. For a few
minutes he remained where he was, and learned a little of
Justine Caine through his eyes. Even now, when she was standing still, her body in its sea-green sheath of a dress seemed to
him alive with the same limber strength and grace that had
entranced him that night in Barcelona when he had lain in wait
for Robert Alvar. Tonight her dark hair was caught up high at the
back of her head. Her features . . . no, she was too far away for
him to see her face clearly, and besides it was turned slightly
away from him as she looked up at and listened to – spoke to,
occasionally, briefly – the tall young man with her. But he
perceived it to be broad at the forehead and fine-boned, and her
eyes were set wide apart beneath straight, dark brows. What
colour were they, he wondered? And were she and the blond
guy actually talking computers, as Ann had suggested? If so,
then computers must be a fascinating subject to Justine Caine,
for she appeared to be enjoying the conversation. But then
Shearer smiled wryly inside. No, that may not be the case, he
was thinking. This woman was an accomplished undercover
agent, indeed she must have been a brilliant and extraordinarily
brave one to have deceived for so long, while working at very
close quarters with, such a street-wise operator as Alvar. To act a
part must come naturally to her. . . . A gift like that, it surely
makes things difficult sometimes for her friends? Would they be
able to distinguish acted-Justine from real-Justine? Would her
lover—?

Angrily, Shearer jerked his eyes away from the woman in the sea-green dress, telling himself he'd come to Jack's party to find out what evidence, *if any*, Justine Caine had for her unofficial suspicions concerning the suicide theory to account for Alvar's death, not to get to know her in any personal sense. Composing himself, he made his way across the room to greet and join a man he knew, Max Hartwell, one of Curtis's neighbours.

It was a move which placed him closer to Justine Caine and facing her directly. Since Hartwell's back was to her, while conversing with him Shearer could occasionally glance beyond him and appraise her more closely. He took full advantage of this, telling himself it was advisable to discover as much as you could about your (possible) enemy; yet at the same time he was aware at some deep and as yet not fully acknowledged level of consciousness that he was looking at her because doing so was giving him intense delight and was creating in him a profound desire, an *intention* almost, to get to know her – not just for his special purpose, but for himself. Her eyes, he observed, were heavy-lidded and amber in colour. Moreover, they had . . . they had *connected* with his own, they had *taken note of him* with a sudden and rawly personal interest. It had happened only the once, a few moments after he had joined Hartwell. She too had looked past the man she was talking with, her eyes had met his own and had locked with them for a second before she returned her gaze to her companion. However in that second the spark had been there, Shearer was sure of it: she was as physically and emotionally aware of him, attracted to him, as he was of her.

Therefore, in a little while, he excused himself from Hartwell and went to her, greeting her by name and apologizing to the computer buff for interrupting. Justine Caine responded courteously, as he had expected she would, whereupon the young man expressed regret for having monopolized her for so long and wandered away.

'How did you know my name?' she asked Shearer then.

'Does it matter?'

She shook her head, the amber eyes intent on his. 'Nevertheless, I'd like to know yours?'

'Shearer. Hal Shearer.' As he spoke, he saw a sudden tension in her, a flicker of wariness – or was it sadness? – shadow her face briefly. 'You're not such a good actress as I thought,' he said.

'What?'

'My name. It . . . worried you. Have you heard it before?'

'Yes.'

'In what context?'

'Mr Shearer, this is not party talk. Let's change the subject.'

'No. Let's change our location. There are certain things I need to talk to you about, I need to do that very much. I'm an old friend of Jack's, I know this house well, and upstairs he's got a small study and when I'm here we use it. You and I could go there now. No one will disturb us. Will you come?'

Up on the first floor, the windows of Jack Curtis's study stood open to the garden at the side of the house. Outside, evening sunlight slanted in across flowerbeds to fetch up against a six-foot stand of runner beans flaring their scarlet blossoms to brilliance. In the small, comfortably furnished room, Justine Caine and Shearer had been talking for almost an hour, she seated in a plump-cushioned, raffishly time-worn armchair, he occasionally perching briefly on the edge of the desk alongside the windows but mostly on the move, padding about the familiar room, halting sometimes to ask her a question or to search her eyes, her face. She had answered his questions freely and, so far as he could judge, with absolute honesty. And he believed now that in all she had told him about what she had observed at the crime scene there was nothing to give him cause for concern. All the evidence she had taken such careful note of at the time pointed to Fuentes having been shot dead in the course of a struggle for possession of the gun, following which Alvar killed himself with the same gun some minutes later. And she had told him that, although she 'had a feeling' that a third person might have been present at the killings – had perhaps even been involved some-how in them – she had absolutely no concrete evidence to support that hypothesis.

But: during the last hour Shearer had realized that there lay between them one final matter he had to find the truth of if, as he increasingly desired should come to pass, he and Justine were to . . . well, to be together in any close way. A mysterious and special sexual rapport had sparked into life between them; he and this woman belonged together, he was sure of it; everything in him – and in her eyes too, now, whenever they met and held his – was telling him so. But that would only ever be possible if she knew the reality of him and was able to accept it. So he had to put the watershed question to her. Only when she had answered that with total truth, together with any more self-revealing and self-penetrating ones which might flow from the answer she gave to it – only then would they both know whether or not they could stay in each other's lives. Therefore he went to stand close in front of her and . . . asked it.

'What is it you know about me, that made you flinch when I told you my name?' he asked.

She did not answer immediately. Looking up at him, she searched his eyes; then a small and secretive smile lengthened her mouth. But it was gone before it had any meaning for him. 'I found out that Elena Fuentes had a contract out on a certain man,' she told him then. 'Fuentes was my "territory", so I took steps to find out the name of that man. It was Shearer.'

'What else did you find out about him, apart from his name?'

'Not much. There wasn't time, our op. was near climax.'

'*What do you know about me*, was what I asked! Answer me!'

She did not move. She smiled up at him, but this smile said with great clarity, *back off!* Take that tone with me and I'll walk away from you.

'I'm sorry.' He ran a hand through his hair and swung aside, went across to the fireplace and stood peering up at an oil painting hung there, a tumultuously dramatic picture of storm off Stark Point on the Devon coast. 'It matters to me, what you know about me,' he said, his back to her.

'Because I'm a policewoman?'

There was that in her voice which made him turn round to face her. 'You know it's not—'

'I do. All the information I have on you, so far, is that you were a police officer, and that Fuentes was gunning for you because twenty years ago you shot her brother dead.'

'You don't know the circumstances of the shooting?'

'No. As I said, there wasn't time, our mission—' She broke off as, suddenly, voices and laughter floated in through the window from the garden below, shattering their absorption in each other. Their heads turned as one and, for a second, they listened to the chit-chat going on in the garden. The subject was cricket, which to some of the group was obviously a matter of serious import whereas to others it apparently served as an opportunty for the delivery of jokey witticisms.

'The party has spilled over from the patio,' Shearer observed then, turning back to Justine Caine. 'You and I, we no longer belong in it, I think? I'd like you to understand about the killing of Elena Fuentes's brother. May I take you to dinner now, so we can talk in privacy?'

'A restaurant? Hardly private—'

'Not a restaurant. I live half-an-hour's drive from here.' The brooding severity of his face relaxed into a smile as he saw the angst fade from her eyes. 'We can sneak down the back stairs, out through the kitchen and round to the cars,' he went on with growing hope. 'I have smoked ham in the fridge, salad and stuff. A bottle of good red wine to hand. Tempted?'

'Already fallen.' She stood up, smoothing the skirt of her sea-green dress into place. 'But isn't it a bit rude? Like slapping one's host in the face?'

Shearer realized she was going with him anyway, whether or not it was discourteous to their host; and he gave a quiet laugh, great pleasure in him that she would leave like this with him, secretly, she and he together as if they lived in a world of their own wherein – hopefully? – each would understand *and accept* the other's self and *mores*, regardless of whether those conformed with currently prevailing opinion.

'Jack probably won't notice, and anyway he wouldn't give a damn if he did,' he said, shutting the window then taking her hand and leading the way out of the room. 'He set this up for me, so I could meet you. He knows everything I'm going to tell you, knows all I've done and why I've done it.'

'Is he the only one who does?'

He closed the door behind them, dropped her hand and faced her. 'Plenty of people know some of it,' he said to her sombrely, 'but there is one whole, separate side of things – *of me* – that only Jack and I know in total. And that side, it's not . . . pretty. Also, it places me outside the law.'

'I've seen a lot of things done which could quite correctly be labelled "unpretty", and some of them were without doubt marginally or not-so-marginally outside the law.' Her eyes did not leave his. 'In my experience, such acts may serve a useful, even necessary purpose. They have to be kept under wraps, though, don't they? To protect the people who've carried them out.'

'Are you good at keeping such things under wraps?'

'This far in my life I've had no problems doing so. To me it's always seemed that the cardinal point is one's own belief in the person who's done the law-breaking. One has to have absolute belief in their integrity. Given that, I go my own way.'

'Regardless of . . . commonly accepted principles?'

For a moment she looked at him in silence. Then a faint smile touched her mouth, her eyes. ' "To one's own self" and all that,' she said lightly. 'You're not the only one around with such a philosophy, you know, *Mister* Shearer.' Then she put her hand in his and together they went downstairs and escaped from Curtis's party through the back door of his house.

25

'Jim Smith, Elena Fuentes's brother, he was a nothing, no more than one of a small drugs-peddling gang one of Alvar's henchmen was running on the side. The night the Specials mounted the raid we weren't after Smith, we were after the two lead players who'd summoned him and his fellow thugs to a meeting. The raid got off to a bad start. The team I was in, three of us, we weren't getting support from where we'd expected it, our back-up hadn't made it on time. No good us waiting, though, we had to press forward fast or the sods we were after would be out and away.' Shearer was standing in the middle of his sitting-room, his back to Justine who was curled into one end of the sofa by the fireplace, watching him, listening to him, her shoes off and her feet up on the dark-red upholstery. He had a glass of red wine in his hand, but he was not drinking from it, he was simply staring down into it. Inside his head he was reliving that night twenty years ago when, in effect, his chosen career had been cut off in the bud; it still had the power to claw him back into its appalling and, finally, bloody chaos.

'All hell broke loose,' he went on, his voice a monotone, low and hard. 'Our lot, we'd forfeited the initiative. I lost contact with my two mates. Suddenly, found myself boxed in, under fire from two sides. Didn't know where my oppos were. Knew I wasn't getting support from them, though. Knew, too, that I'd got to get mobile and do my job quick or the whole op. would fold. To do that I'd got to put out of action one of the two villains who'd got me pinned down. So I chose my target and – went for him, out of cover, gunning for him.'

Slowly then Shearer turned to Justine. But, as he finished what he had to say, his eyes were still on the red wine in his glass. 'The one I shot was Jim Smith, brother to Helen Smith as she was then, before she married. I aimed to disable him but . . . I killed him. He died in hospital later that night.'

He'd made no attempt to escape blame, she noticed, hadn't offered any of the excuses there'd probably been, such as target moving in the last split second, or bad light. She did not refer to them either. She simply asked him if he'd been sacked.

'Not exactly,' he answered. 'It was made plain to me that I'd be back on the beat if I stayed on, with my prospects for the future blighted to say the least. I resigned.'

'The raid as a whole, was it rated a success?'

'Initially, yes. We got both the lead guys we were after.' For the first time since he had started his story, Shearer looked directly at her. 'There followed a high-profile trial. It resulted in both men being freed on a legal technicality,' he said bleakly.

'Christ!'

Her appalled exclamation, and the expression on her face, seemed to him somehow to comprehend and contain all the despair, all the anger and bitter frustration which had stormed through him and possessed him on the day he had heard that judgment handed down. He placed his glass on a nearby table, went across to the sofa and sat down at the other end of it. 'That day I changed for ever,' he said to her, his voice level, a cold resentful pride in his face. 'That day I reasoned my way to personal convictions I was prepared to live by at any cost whatsoever – somewhat grim convictions by most people's standards, I think. Ten years went by before I was in a position to do anything practical about converting that mental commitment into action – I had to earn my living, and reacquire some status in life. But the day those two drug-dealers walked free was the day it all began.'

Inside Justine's head, a horde of questions was clamouring to be asked but she voiced none of them. There was within her a peculiar exaltation, for she had realized Hal Shearer was about to make her privy to *the actual, lived results* of that long-past decision of his to 'translate into action' his discovered convictions. He'd only ever confided so much to one other person, namely Jack Curtis, he'd told her earlier. That he should place such trust in her, so soon, moved her deeply. And with a quick stirring of the heart she took his trust for her own and vowed hers to him in return. The giving and the taking will make me part of him, she thought, and I want that. Why? No, don't ask. Just accept and be glad of it. Take the gift, woman. Take it with both hands but ... carefully. Rare and precious gifts break easily. Also, remember that when you accept a gift you are implicitly accepting its consequent responsibilities.

'Drug abuse, together with the criminality which feeds it and feeds *on* it are, I believe, one of the greatest evils facing us now,' he went on. 'All the way along the line, from production, it corrupts and brutalizes.'

'Agreed. But people assume it's being dealt with by the appropriate bodies and let it lie unchallenged—'

'I've been challenging it for the last ten years,' he interrupted quietly. 'In my own small but, to me, infinitely satisfying way.'

'*How?*' Sliding her legs off the sofa she sat forward, staring at him. 'In God's name, *how?*'

But suddenly Shearer experienced a flicker of doubt: so soon, to lay himself open to this woman so recently met? This *police-woman* so recently met? He prevaricated. 'The way the trade in narcotics is being *legally* opposed at present isn't achieving enough,' he said. 'It's managing to keep the lid on the problem, just about and on the whole—'

'That's true. But what I asked you was, what you yourself are doing, and have been doing, about it? You, personally?'

For a long moment he sat silent, searching her eyes. And as he was doing so, from some subliminal depths of his being a warning flashed up into his full consciousness and prophesied, *if you cannot tell this woman the unalloyed truth of yourself you will lose her–*

'Are you afraid to tell me?' Roughly, her voice cut across his thoughts.

He saw anger in her eyes. It filled him with elation, that she, too, cared so much. 'I go straight for the principals driving and profiting from the trade,' he said.

' "Go for"?'

'Kill. That way they can't walk free from a court of law.'

She stiffened. Her eyes widened, but they did not run away from his. 'Alvar?' she asked. Saw him nod and went on, 'There have been others, then?'

'Alvar was the fourth to pay what I consider to be a fair price.'

'That's moral arrogance!'

'Perhaps. But as I see it, it's no more than justice on each one of them.' Then what he was seeing in her face gave him hope. 'I think you'd find there's a lot of victims out there who'd agree with me on that,' he added quietly.

Getting to her feet, Justine walked across to the windows and stood looking out. What lay out there was a far cry from beautiful, the apartments on his side of the block offering as they did panoramic views of a highly developed area; but as she stared across the spread of shopping malls, business zones and residential sectors, all linked together by a comprehensive road system, it seemed to her that the whole was possessed of the particular beauty born of belonging to the act of living, of being throbbingly vivid with life. It wasn't all sweetness and light out there, of course not; it could be and doubtless frequently was dull, tragic or whatever, she knew that well enough. But the people-living vitality of it was always pulsing away out there and that gave it something, a quality of value, didn't it? People are people and therefore are infinitely different, infinitely fascinating . . . and the motivations driving their lives are infinitely diverse.

She turned away from the window. Shearer had not moved so she went to him. 'Alvar, will he be the last?' she asked. 'Are you going to stop now?'

'If I say no, will you shop me?'

'I would never shop you, and you know it. But I think you should stop now. Before it's too late.'

'Too late for what?'

'You. *You, Hal Shearer.*' But she saw a guarded look slide in across his eyes and moved away from that, telling herself there would be time for it later, he and she had time. Sure of that now, she smiled at him. 'Do you know what I'd like to do now?' she asked.

'How should I? Tell me.'

'First, I'd like for us to eat some of that smoked ham you said you had here, and drink this wine. Then I'd like us to brew a large pot of coffee, bring it in here, and sit down on the sofa again.'

'And?' he prompted her silence.

'Then we drink the coffee and *you tell me.* About Alvar and the other three of his kind. Tell me, in full detail, the reason for, and the circumstances of, their deaths.'

'What if I decline?'

'Then I will leave now. In declining you will have shut me out of your life, lumped me in with the rest of the world; so there'd be no point in my staying.'

He got to his feet and stared her in the eyes. For a moment she thought he was going to kiss her, he stood so close. But he did not. 'The ham really is good,' he said. 'It was smoked at a little place up in Herefordshire, speciality of a man who farms near Glaslyn, my home. The kitchen here, it's quite big, we can eat in there. Come.' He reached out and touched her shoulder.

Epilogue

Three months later

White walled, and roofed in the local Menorcan style with convex-concave terracotta tiles, the single-storey villa stood alone, nestled under the crest of the hill sloping down to a narrow beach edging the cove 200 feet below. It was a small place, built for summer living but nevertheless acknowledging the ferocity of the Mediterranean's spring and winter storms: sturdy wooden shutters protected the four large glass doors which opened out from its main room on to a broad veranda facing the sea. These were folded back now, and leaning on the balustrade edging the veranda, Shearer breathed the warm quiet of the late September evening deep into his lungs and looked around him. To his left, rugged coast stretched away towards Grau and the north-east of the island. A half-mile to his right, the fishing village of Cala Mesquida banded the crescent bay, guarded on a rocky promontory by a ruined Moorish fort. Looking out to sea, Shearer gave silent thanks to Justine Caine's brother who had loaned them the villa – inherited from an uncle who'd bought it in the late fifties. They had been there a fortnight.

'Only one more day here.' Arriving at his side, Justine leaned her forearms on the balustrade, one bare elbow touching his, amber eyes pensive. She was wearing a shirt of his and little else.

Not looking at her he thought, *now, this evening*. It has to be decided between us *now*. Three months we gave ourselves that night two weeks after Jack's party when we slept together for the first time. Three months to live together without any more discussion regarding my self-awarded warrant to deliver 'justice' to top-dog purveyors of narcotics operating outside the law; we both knew we'd said all there was to say, at the time, on that subject. Well, today is the last day of those three months and there isn't a lot of it left. As soon as we get back to London she returns to work.

'Let's get it settled, Justine, settled one way or the other,' he said. 'Will you stay with me?'

'Will you swear off your private war?' she countered, having been thinking along similar lines as he.

For a while he was silent, gazing out across the sea. Then he said quietly, ' "Stop before it's too late", you said to me the evening of Jack's party. Remember? "Too late for *you*, Hal Shearer".'

'You knew what I meant by that, you knew *all* I meant. So I'm asking you, will you stop now?'

Slowly, he said, 'I swear to you I will stop.'

'For the rest of your given life?'

'Yes.' But he sensed she wanted more from him.

She did. 'Tell me why, please.'

He thought about it. But at the end of his thinking all he gave her were almost accusing questions. 'What is it you want from me? Confession to some Damascene conversion?'

'Not necessarily, Hal. Simply the truth. I take it you know the truth?'

'I know the truth all right! The reason is simply because I

know damn well that's the only way I'll get you!'

It was cruelly said, and she let a silence lie between them. Then she said, softly, 'Well, you've got me.'

But he was not ready for it, quite. 'And . . . the past, Justine?' he asked, keeping his eyes on the sea. 'Four men dead by my hand. Are you sure you can live with that fact – undamaged by it – for the rest of *your* life?'

She turned to him then, smiling. 'Hal Shearer,' she said, putting her hands on his shoulders and pulling him round to face her. 'Hal Shearer, are you really a bird of such little brain? I've just *told* you I can! Do you want it in words of one syllable? In writing, maybe?'

'Christ, I'm a fool, aren't I?' A deep joy in him he circled his arm round her waist. 'So you'll marry me?'

'Tomorrow if that were possible.'

'And as of this moment I declare my vendetta at an end.'

'Successfully concluded, would you say?'

A sudden bleakness hardened his face. Looking away, he considered it. 'No,' he said finally. 'But then in reality it's a war that's unlikely to be totally and for ever finished, isn't it? It's a long, hard slog, a highly sophisticated campaign that has to be fought on many fronts; and it's not for one man to attempt to tackle in his own way. I accept that now.'

'That's a big thing you've given me. I've got something to say to you, too, before we leave this behind and get on with being us. It's this: I am glad you killed Robert Alvar.'

Shearer pulled her close to him. 'Say that again,' he whispered, his mouth close to her hair. 'Give it to me just once more and then he's gone for ever.'

'I am glad you killed Robert Alvar.'

'Thank you for that,' he said. 'But I regret Elena's death. In a strange way, I owed her.'

'Owed her? Because of her brother, you mean? I don't see—'

But Shearer had long determined to keep faith with Helen and James Smith. 'Yes, for her brother,' he said. And left it at that.

B3
B7